To Play or Not to Play

A Romance Novel

Standalone Book One of the Romance Romp Series

Emily Bow

To Play or Not to Play
Copyright April 2018

For information about permission to reproduce selections from this book, write to Emily@EmilyBow.com.

For upcoming books and other information, visit www.EmilyBow.com.

[1. Fiction 2. Romance 3. Contemporary 4. New Adult
5. Romantic Comedy 6. ChickLit]

Chapter 1

Yep, I was in a public building, and I was going to take my shirt off. I wish I could say I was on a wild graduation trip, but I wasn't.

I was late for my summer internship with the British government, and I was still in my travel clothes. In England, clothes matter. So, yoga pants and a t-shirt weren't going to cut it. I needed to put on my suitable pink suit dress and look sensible. The Brits were all about sense and sensibility.

My practical side warred with my sneaky side. Should I do this?

I'd endured a nine-hour flight with security screens at the airport and here at the Prime Minister's residence. Then, I'd followed the guards' directions, but I hadn't found the Interns' Session room. Instead, I'd found a narrow back hallway that smelled like apple cleaning product and emptiness.

I couldn't fix being late, but I could end this jetlagged walk of shame—me here, wearing the same clothes from the night before.

I was out of time, a little lost, and there was no one else here. So, why not? A pleased rush flitted through me at the solution. I toyed with the hem of my shirt.

I'd wear the dress Mom had picked out for me back in Houston. As if I didn't know what to wear on the first day of a job. I was twenty-one, a college graduate. I knew how to appear professional. I jostled the dress I carried over my arm, undid the modesty hook at the top, and yanked down the zipper. I'd throw the dress over what I was wearing and then yank off my yoga pants from underneath.

So wrong. So, so wrong. Doing an inappropriate quick change to meet modesty standards.

I was doing it.

I shimmied my dress on over my clothes.

Whew. The dress was on. Unzipped. But on.

I quickly shucked my yoga pants and stuffed them into my overlarge purse.

Success.

I reached behind me and shoved my t-shirt down so it wouldn't get caught in the zipper track. Heat hit me from my exertions. Wearing this dress over a t-shirt would be warm. I'd be uncomfortable, overstuffed all day. Especially here in England, a country that had minimal air conditioning. Some called Texas over-air-conditioned, but I knew the truth. No one else air conditioned enough.

So...

Why not? I let the front of my dress hang down so that I was essentially wearing a t-shirt and a skirt. I crossed my arms over my chest, grabbed the hem of my t-shirt, got it up and over... and... I pulled. My hair yanked; my charm bracelet caught in the strands.

I was stuck. And the position hurt.

Ring…ring. The mechanical buzz of my phone jolted me, reminding me that other people existed.

I pulled the top of the dress up over my bra. With my right arm holding up my dress and my left arm stuck in the air, I had no hand to answer the call.

On the upside, the gaping back of my dress made the room cooler.

Ring…ring… My sister's ringtone sang out. I couldn't believe Felicity was calling to bug me. She wasn't even in the same time zone. It was probably 2 AM where she was.

Ring…ring. Ring…ring.

I kicked my purse like that would help. The yoga pants fell out along with half my stuff. Lip balm, an eye mask, the dirty book I was reading. It all clattered out of the purse and onto the floor, joining me in this ridiculous dance.

Steps sounded on the marble.

Crap. Crap. Crap. I jerked my head like my dog. Trapper did that right before he went still and then started barking like crazy at whoever had come to the door. I now knew what he had felt in those moments. Dread, interest, and a fierce determination to state that this was my territory.

Because here I was, half out of this dress and no way to get into it fast. Being stuck like this in a mall dressing room was annoying. Being half naked in a public foyer was panic inducing. Full on, heart-in-my-throat panic. That panic shot adrenaline through my veins and pumped anxiety through every inch of me.

Someone was coming. Solid steps. Not the light clicking of heels. It had to be a guy.

The steps stopped.

He. Was. Here.

I could see him. And he could see me. A lot of me.

He was fair-haired, tall. My age. Another intern maybe? My heart thumped impossibly harder. He was tourist brochure handsome.

"Well," he said, sounding surprised and, I don't know, intrigued?

Stop worrying about him. Think. Fix the situation. Process my strengths.

The guy was late. Like me. Not where he was supposed to be. Like me. It gave me an edge over him, as much of an edge as I could grab at this moment. I knew how to take an advantage when I found one.

He was still staring at me, and a flush hit the top of his cheekbones. The blush, the tamed haircut, and the pressed navy suit belied his feral blue eyes. His gaze was fixed on me as if I were performing this arms-overhead inadvertent belly dance for his benefit.

I yanked at my arm. My hair pulled. I winced and maneuvered my arm into an angle I never wanted to feel again. Holding in the groan, I tried not to yank all my hair out. My American outrage roiled. This wasn't how today was supposed to go.

The guy lifted his hand, held up his pointer finger to the left, and opened his mouth.

Dude was about to give me directions. I yanked my arm left. My hair pulled harder. A garbled yelp left my lips. "Grrr. Ouch."

His pointed directions had not helped.

The clatter of dress shoes and a babble of voice came from down the hall. Great. Now I'd found the interns. Or a group of ambassadors. Or the press. All of them could be coming this way and see me stuck like this. My arm overhead, and my dress hanging open on my first day.

Nooo.

Alarm crashed through me. I stared into his bright blue eyes. He'd failed me once with his inadequate finger pointing, but I had no other choice but to seek his assistance. Fast.

"Help me." Half plea, half demand, the words were clear, but I jiggled my body again in case he was slow to understand the situation. Fresh pain arced through my skull, and I held in a yelp.

He glanced down the hall, taking in the imminent arrival of the horde. Their voices were loud and eager. Had to be the other college interns. Interns who'd give me a stripper nickname that would last longer than this summer. It would haunt me for life. That was this moment.

"Please."

He rushed forward and scooped up my stuff.

My yoga pants and lipstick! Was he kidding? My shoulders slumped, and my arm jerked, making my eyes sting at the painful pull. I was standing here like a half-transitioned shape-shifting unicorn, like in the novel I was reading, and he was gathering my spilled belongings. Bottled water. Eye drops. Plastic zip bag of hard candy. The book cover with the entwined couple inside a heart and two unicorns shimmering in the background.

Stop.

Please stop.

Didn't he know? No girl wanted someone to pick up her private purse items. Ever. Who knew what I'd left in there?

He got it all though. Scooped it up without hesitation and stood in front of me, blocking me from the newcomers. He took a step closer, backing me toward the yellow wall. My butt hit the white trim.

He patted behind me, and a small coat closet opened. There hadn't been a doorknob there. I'd have seen it. The front door to Number 10 hadn't had a knob either. What was wrong with doorknobs? This was so British. Only if you were in-the-know could you get in. We shifted inside, and he pulled the door closed, securing us in the privacy of a cloak closet.

Safe. Secure. Private.

Finally. Relief hit me, and I closed my eyes. We stayed quiet.

Steps sounded louder.

The guy slid his warm, large hands over my raised arm.

My eyelids popped open, but it was too dark in here to see him. I could just feel him.

He worked at my charm bracelet and pulled the cotton t-shirt from my wrist.

He'd freed me. I shook out my arm and rolled my shoulders. Lovely.

I turned my back to him and put my arms through the armholes. The dress was on now. "Zip me up," I whispered, keeping quiet so the outsiders wouldn't hear me.

He put his hands on my waist, felt for the zipper with his calloused, strong fingers, and slid it up the tracks to the top. My breath caught with the motion, as if he were zipping up my ability to take in air. His warm fingers glanced over my back. Zings and shivers joined us in the small closet.

It just got weird.

Warm, exhilarating, and intense. More intense than my last make-out session with my ex-boyfriend, which was crazy. My breath slowed. I breathed in his cologne. He smelled yum. Clean and… I don't know…exciting? I licked my lips and turned to face him.

Chapter 2

We were in the still darkness of the closet together.

I couldn't see him.

I wasn't touching him.

I could just tell he was there. Tall. Solid. Present. Just him and me. The footsteps became a white noise concealing us. Just us. Alone. Together.

More.

Did he deserve a kiss of thanks?

He did, or I just had to get closer, and this was going to be my excuse. I slid my arm around his neck and raised up to put my mouth to his ear. He smelled great, clean and masculine and like something I wanted. "Thank you," I whispered.

He bent toward me.

Yeah, he was sending me a signal. I slid my lips over his cheek. Half a thank you, half to see how it felt.

Who was I kidding? Totally to see how it felt. It made all those panicked feelings float away, melting into a delicious warmth and leaving behind an ache.

I wanted more.

I wanted his lips on mine. His hands back on my waist. On me. I inched closer.

"I'm missing one." A female voice sounded through the door—my age, peeved.

It jolted me out of my stirring moment, and I let go of the guy. He put his hands on my waist as if to keep me. I liked that. Warm strong guy-hands that made electricity flow through me in the dark.

"Shouldn't I have been notified by now? That would have been appropriate, don't you think?" the voice asked, clearly berating someone else.

Their presence put a damper on my moment.

Two people were out there. Lingering and griping like no one had given them their morning tea or it had been under-steeped and weak. That would probably be part of my job—to tote tea. I hoped it wouldn't be for the griper.

I had a suspicion that she was Peppa, the head intern, and I was the "missing" intern. Or…maybe she had the numbers wrong. Two people were missing. Him and me. The guy in here with me had been late, too.

They were probably mostly talking about him.

Yeah, it was him.

A desire to slip into the crowd outside and leave him to take the blame for being late flitted through me. He was late, too. He deserved it.

He brushed his fingers back and forth on my upper arm in a small motion. Comforting, a turn-on…both. No way I'd screw him over. He was late because he'd helped me. I owed him. And, I could save him. "Stay here," I whispered. "I'll move her away, and you can get out."

I stepped toward the door, the motion shaky. My shakiness was due to jetlag, adrenaline, or hunger. Or maybe it was this encounter with him. My lips on his cheek. So close to his mouth. If Peppa hadn't arrived... I would have taken it a step further. He wasn't mine. Not my boyfriend, not even a date, but I would have.

I had to go. I didn't want to. But I had no choice. I drew in a breath and slipped out the door, leaving my filmy t-shirt, a bit of dignity, and him behind.

I was out of the closet, but I wasn't ready to face the consequences of my lateness. I blinked against the light. Not that the Brits used bright lights, but after the dark closet, the mild hallway lighting hit my eyes hard. Like when I changed a light bulb and knew to look away, but I didn't. I walked across the small side foyer where the griper was going at it with another lady.

Closer. Closer.

I didn't want to chat with those two. I was hungry, tired, and not eager, but I had to do it for the guy I left behind.

A little bird popped out of the mahogany cuckoo clock, marking 9:30 AM, making sure they knew I was late. The interns were supposed to meet Peppa in the sessions hall at 9 AM GMT sharp. Peppa was going to judge me for being late. The wigged guy in the portrait behind her sure was.

The other interns were disappearing up the hall. I could catch them, blend right in. Half of me wanted to. But that would leave the hot guy trapped.

I sighed and followed the maroon floor runner over to Peppa and the lady she was berating. I strove to stir up some enthusiasm and energy. Bracing myself, I smiled one of those big, all-teeth smiles, one too big for this early hour. "Hi.

Looking for me? I'm Kira Kitman. I couldn't find the sessions hall." I looked straight into Peppa's gray eyes as I half-lied.

"I'm called Peppa." Peppa was shorter than me, but she did one of those sweeping looks, checking out my appearance from my ballet flats to my tied-up brunette hair. I could only imagine how great my hair looked after all my maneuvers. Her English-gray gaze assured me it was a mess.

Whatever. I tucked in a loose strand.

Peppa smiled a small smile like she'd won and arched her thin blonde eyebrows. "You're late, you know. Did you go to Number Five Downing Street instead?" She snickered to herself like she'd made a joke and turned to the other lady, who smiled back at her but didn't really look as if she got the joke either. She looked back at me. "Did you even think to ask someone where to go? Read the map in the packet? That would have been the appropriate thing to do."

I sucked in a breath through my nose and didn't answer the rhetorical question. Wasn't her job to welcome me, make me comfortable, and *then* lecture me about it? That's what would have happened at home. *Well, bless your heart. Those airlines. Can I get you a glass of tea? Now, you know, if you'd set your alarm a little earlier…*

I shook my head out of Texas culture. I was in England. Things would be different, colder, more confusing, but I'd get it eventually.

I turned to the shorter lady beside Peppa, hinting for an introduction. She was dark-complexioned, and her big brown eyes looked relieved that I was there. Probably because it took Peppa's focus off her.

The lady said, "I'll ensure the room's sorted." Then she scampered off.

Yeah, scampered, like a bunny breaking for the open fields.

"You weren't here at nine?" Peppa stated more than asked.

Again with that? I strove to lighten the mood. "There was no handle on the front door." The black steel door of Number 10 was famous for not having a handle.

"That's because it cannot be opened from the outside." Peppa smiled tightly. "We don't let just anyone in." She checked her list. "You're the last of the interns. American." Peppa checked her tablet again. If I was the last one on the list, why was she still checking the tablet? Her morning must've been going as poorly as mine. Her words were tight, and I didn't know if my American nationality or my tardiness caused the disapproval. Lateness in Britain was a sin. They didn't have the same five-minute grace period allowed in America. And apparently, this was really bugging her.

Peppa smelled like disapproval, cucumbers, and rosemary. Why would she buy perfume that smelled like a garnish? I don't know. Mine was a pear-honey note perfume I'd gotten for Christmas when we came over to see my grandparents. I didn't love it, but I could shop for a new one here. One to remember my summer by. Scent and memory are linked. Like that guy's cologne. If I got a whiff of it again, that lovely showered-guy-and-ocean cologne, I'd be transported right back to the closet. Lovely.

Peppa cleared her throat as a hint that it was my turn to engage in this terrific conversation.

"Here to serve." My voice came out husky from early morning disuse. I knew I should have flown in the day before, but I hadn't wanted to leave America any sooner than I had to. I also knew I should be grateful for this opportunity, but I'd wanted a White House internship, and my twin had tricked me out of it. Now, I was here. In my dress. Ready to go. Hiding a guy in a closet.

It was life in the dorm all over again. Though it had never been me hiding a guy. I hadn't been ready to go there until my last boyfriend. I didn't want to think about him now. I had to move Peppa away, so this guy could escape without her notice. "What are the odds of my getting breakfast?" Yeah, I was hungry enough to put it out there. I was that weird jetlag hungry. I didn't know if I wanted toast or a steak or both. Two birds, one stone. I'd eat and save the guy. Pancakes, maple syrup, melted butter… My stomach rumbled. "Anyone here big on waffles?"

Peppa didn't coo over my hunger or feed me like a Texan would have. She drew in a sharp breath and shook her head. "Breakfast ended at 8:30 for those who were here." Her blonde bob fell in front of her eyes, and she tucked it behind her ear, showing her perfect skin and minimal makeup, making her appear more like she was my age.

Weird how we'd probably both just graduated college and she looked corporate-sophisticated and corporate-angry already. I didn't know what I looked like, but it wasn't that. I undid my hairclip and re-spun my hair up in it.

Peppa eyed me like I'd flipped up my skirt and straightened my garter. "The assignments are being given out in the state dining room. As stated." Peppa pointed a buffed, unpainted fingernail toward the yellow corridor. "So, that's where you should be. Don't you think?"

Oh, I thought a lot of things. I finished off my hair and turned that way. "Are they?" Whatever. Look at her buffed nails. My nails would never be unpainted. Even chipped and in need of a file, there would still be color. Me and my painted nails would tote papers to ambassadors. That was going to be my summer job. "I already know my assignment. Paper Runner. Assigned to the American Ambassador." I tried to make my voice sound enthused, because what choice was there? That's the kind of assignment they gave graduates with literature degrees. Errand runners. Yay.

My exhaustion was sucking my mood down like quicksand, and it was getting hard to fake it. I pulled out the toothy smile again, wishing I had some Vaseline to slick on my teeth as a reminder to grin, like beauty contestants used. Beauty contestants, and people who worked with Peppa.

Peppa's mouth pinched. She saw through me.

I dragged from my purse the security badge the guard had given me. The photo showed me, all travel weary. My hair was in its messy brunette bun, my eyes shadowed. Had I known they'd snap photos on day one, I would have done my makeup on the plane. I should have known. Same as school badges and job badges—photos get taken early, when you least want them. When a combination of sick anxiety had kept you up all night and uncertainty over what to wear had left you a bit off.

I was so off today. I clipped the badge to my collar—yep, this dress had a Peter Pan collar. Wearing the badge made me official though. Hopefully, it would stop Peppa from looking at me like she could throw me out. That'd be the quickest roundtrip ever.

Peppa nodded at my name badge. "I'll be looking into your assignment. Jobs aren't final until you arrive. The packet said that."

And there had been a packet. A paper packet. Very old school. And a giant PDF in an email. Page one had clearly stated my job—Paper Runner. I had read as far as page one. Now she was implying I might not be a Paper Runner.

Jeez. My assignment couldn't be worse than that.

Could it?

A tingling of anxiety shoved at the jetlag and a desire to defend myself rose with it. "The plane was late. Blame your airline." Oh. I knew the Southern 'You catch more flies with honey' behavior rule, but I ignored it. I ignored that truth because pleasantries were lost on people like Peppa. She was like a kitchen garbage disposal for pleasantries. I could tell. My efforts would've been wasted, crushed up, and washed away.

Peppa's mouth curved at my response, my defensiveness. She'd sensed weakness.

I reined in my ill temper. *Don't make an enemy here.* That would make this one long London summer. I shifted on my feet and hiked my purse strap higher.

Say something nice.

I could think of nothing. What a welcome. This was on her. "Point me toward the sessions room. Please." I knew I sounded grumpy but couldn't make myself stop. Low blood sugar, a lack of sleep, and Peppa trying to control me stoked my temper.

"You'll want to go in the back so as not to disturb." Peppa checked her computer. "Go through the double doors from the small dining room into the state dining room to get your assignment and room sorted." She pointed again and stared at me until I moved.

Rude pointer. Rebellion stirred in my American heart,

but I fought it down and headed out without saying anything.

I should have looked at the map, which was probably page two of the packet. I took directions from a guard after going the wrong way, twice. Once I reached the right hallway, the dining room was easy enough to find.

I went through a metal detector and two more security checkpoints. Both areas had been very modern compared to this room. Golden wood paneling covered the walls of the small dining room and the floor. Yellow-and-cream-striped curtains matched the striped fabric on the chairs. And most importantly, a table had been set at the far end with food, juice, and coffee. I was in the right spot. Me and one other intern.

The guy from the closet stood beside the table. He'd made it out.

I smiled. He was going to be so grateful to me. I strode forward.

He placed a triangular scone onto his plate.

Breakfast and him. Success.

I moved in. "Hi." A tray of picked-over light brown pastries faced me. Scones: dry, dense. I shuddered and snagged one. "Be careful with these. You could chip a tooth." Who knew what kind of overseas dentistry he'd find here? I owed him the warning after his lending me a hand this morning. Not that I wouldn't have gotten out of it on my own. I would have. If anything, he'd hampered me and made me think crazy thoughts. I breathed in, taking in the breakfast aromas. My emotions and my body were totally under my control now.

The guy arched an eyebrow slightly darker than his golden hair.

Whoa. He was attractive. Model handsome. And that

look. It must've been his signature expression. I stepped closer. He had half a foot on me and was built beneath his navy blazer. *Hello.* I had to know more. *Who are you and where are you from?* "Was your flight late, too?"

He looked me over in that guy way, with wicked, wild blue eyes. His gaze lingered on my chest, which he'd seen quite a bit of this morning.

My insides trembled. Maybe it was hunger. Maybe it was jetlag. But that wild look called to me, and my heart pounded to build up blood flow to run to him. My muscles tightened, and my legs turned to jelly. *Come on, gravity, come on, scone, hold me down.* My reaction to him was ridiculous. The scone crumbled in my fingers.

He shook his head, making his blond hair, overlong on top, slide in front of his face, and he turned his attention back to the food.

Okay. No love connection on his end.

Yet.

I was hungry, too. He didn't own the table. Hunger pounded on the walls of my empty belly. My sick reaction to him had just been hunger. That happened. I placed the scone on a china saucer. That was another difference from America. We typically used paper plates—decorated paper plates, but paper nonetheless. But hey, we recycled.

My stomach ached, but I still wasn't eager to bite into the scone. Eyeing the other option, a tureen of breakfast beans, I gave in. I broke off a corner and chewed on the dry, barely sweet pastry. Just like Mom used to make.

He was watching me. I could feel his gaze.

"That's not how you eat a scone," he said in a clear British accent.

I tilted my head. Growing up in Texas with a British mom, I'd heard my fair share of English accents. More than my fair share. His voice was something else. Educated. Contained. The opposite of his wild eyes.

American Eagle, help me, but it worked for me.

He took the broken piece of scone from my fingers. Just that light touch made me hold in a shiver. He slid a butter knife covered in red jam through the middle and scooped a fluff of white cream on top. He held it out to me. His gemstone blue eyes went to my hand, meaning for me to take the scone.

I leaned forward and bit into it while he held it.

Just like a bride with her groom.

Yum.

Chapter 3

Strawberry jam. Cream. Yum. The sugary rush of pleasure hit my taste buds, distracting me from eyeing him like I wanted to taste him, too. The scone was good this way. Great, actually. "Mmm," I said around the small mouthful. The sound contained as much surprise as it did appreciation. "Delicious."

His gaze went to my mouth, and his impossibly bright blue eyes glinted.

I checked for contacts but couldn't discern any edges. Those blue eyes were all his. And he was going to be all mine. I was here for six weeks. I could make that happen. My thoughts should have shocked me, and maybe when I got over the jetlag, they would. But for now, they didn't. He was an unexpected summer treat, and I wanted him. I was weirdly certain about that.

I took the scone from his unresisting fingers. Ooh, la, la. Had we been lying against some British-blue pillows while he handed me this, now that would have been a morning. "Who knew the British could cook? My mom's British, and she can't cook or bake. And she never serves scones like this. Never."

He handed me a glass of milk. "Mine doesn't cook either."

The milk was room temperature, as expected given the unnatural British fondness for warm drinks. Temperature aside, the drink was rich, creamier than white milk back home and somehow better. Delectable.

I nodded toward the double doors that went into the state dining room. I couldn't hear anything from the other side. That was either due to British restraint or because they hadn't started yet. "What are you in for? Which group?" I eyed him up and down. Intelligent. Athletic. Gorgeous. *Visit the British Isles.* "I'm guessing Tourism?"

He frowned and shook his head.

"Public Relations? Paper Runner?" My voice showed my doubt.

"Household," he said.

That was the worst. I grimaced for him as I finished off the last bite of the newly yummy scone. Who knew? Douse a dry rock with cream and jam, have a hot guy hand it to me, and a scone became a treat. My day was looking up. My summer was looking up. Way up.

Hunger abated, I wiped my fingers on a white cloth napkin and glanced at the door before sharing my thoughts. "The household's the worst internship job. You must have signed up later than me." The taunt in my voice shouted *sucker* at him. Guys liked a challenge, and I wanted to challenge him.

"The Prime Family's lovely." His voice was dry and rehearsed. "A wonderful example for Britain."

Prime. Ha. "The Prime Family? That's what we're calling them?" I took another drink of milk and smiled, my mood restored. "You're going to end up babysitting their lovely darlings. Maybe changing nappies." I nodded toward the table. "Or milking their long-haired cows and boiling bottles over a gas flame."

"Doubtful." His face scrunched in manly disapproval. "How old do you think their children are?"

No clue. I hadn't bothered with the reading material. I was lucky I could even name the British Prime Minister and doubted many other Americans could do as well, much less name their offspring. I hadn't planned to come here. When my sister tricked me into the internship, I'd been so angry, I'd refused to look at the material or do research on what an internship for the British government would entail. I knew I should do it, but I couldn't make myself. Pretty much all I knew right now was that I was at Number 10 Downing Street, home and office of the British Prime Minister.

"Any other stereotype you want to hit?" he asked, like he wanted to pull me back from my thoughts, like he wanted my attention on him.

I'd play. "Maybe you'll get to hold their umbrellas. Pet their short-legged Corgis. Or sniff disdainfully at their enemies."

He laughed, a quick short laugh, and his eyes flashed, showing off that wicked light.

I loved it. The wild look made my insides melt and made me want to make him laugh again. *Think. Think.* I could spin *keeping calm and carrying on.*

He looked at me expectantly, not yet reining the wild back in.

Heels sounded against the floor outside the doorway, clicking, and then muted by the rug. I hated that we were being interrupted.

Peppa stood in the doorway like a PE coach with a clipboard. Who used those anymore? She did.

The thin older lady beside her was middle-aged. She wore a suit, looked super polished, and didn't pay us any attention. She focused on her smartphone like someone with places to be.

Peppa focused on us. She stiffened. "Wythe." She nodded to the guy with familiarity and a slight bit of deference—clearly due to his hotness. He was worth appreciating.

Wythe. That was his name. She said it almost like *with*. I had no doubt that when I'd say it, I would drawl it out more like *Y-ath*. I couldn't think of an excuse to say it aloud just then, but I wanted to.

Wythe nodded but took his plate over to a table and chairs. He glanced briefly at the older woman and then dug into his breakfast as if we weren't there. Isolating himself in a room of people. Weird talent. I so wanted to join him.

Peppa looked at me with her control-freak gray eyes. The color of rain on a sidewalk. What was that smell of rain called? Petrichor? She had petrichor eyes. "Kira. You should really go into the session now. Really." Her voice held a tight edge, and her nostrils flared like Trapper's did when I held up a smelly dog bone. Peppa wanted me to leave her alone with the cute Wythe.

No.

Darn it. Okay. I owed her after my stellar entrance. But just an apology. I didn't owe her the guy. Grr. Now I was Trapper, possessive over the tempting bone. "Sorry about before." I shrugged. "Jetlag. Shouldn't have taken it out on you."

Peppa's petrichor gaze didn't shift away. "These things have a way of working themselves out." She crossed the room and opened one of the double doors, and a rush of sound came through. She made a shooing motion like I was a cow balking at the gate. "It would be appropriate for you to go in now."

People who said the words and did the motions. Yuck. The control freak had forced my hand. I scooted inside like a herded cow, and Peppa shut the door behind me, not following. Yep, Peppa wanted to be alone with the gorgeous Wythe, and she'd taken her shot. Oh, well, I would keep calm and carry on by myself. *Farewell, my love.* I'd catch him around the house while toting an attaché case of important papers, while he was toting a diaper bag. I wouldn't let that interfere with my view of his manliness. *Blow up those gender norms, Britain.*

Wythe.

I'd find him again. I'd make a point of it.

In front of me, the room was packed with about fifty interns, all about to blow their summer after college. Half were guys, half girls, all early to mid-twenties, all wearing suits or conservative dresses. My modest pink dress fit in perfectly. I swiped at my hair, making sure the strands were tucked in.

There was an empty seat in the front row, same as there would've been in America. Though the chairs were smaller, wooden, and worn. I strode up there and scooted over to the empty seat. "Pardon me. Sorry." I'd picked up the use of *sorry* from Mom and knew I sounded right at home.

I took an open chair by a lanky guy in a navy suit. He wore his name badge centered on his left jacket pocket and had an eager-to-learn look.

I pulled out my phone.

The guy shifted toward me.

Was he annoyed I was late? Please. No one here was doing anything but chatting.

He got closer, somehow revealing he'd worn too much woodland cologne and not enough shower. My scone turned over in my stomach. Dude, extra cologne never covered up the fact that you skipped your shower. Never ever. Meet people. Shower that morning. Simple math. No wonder he was on time.

I angled slightly away and checked my phone notifications. There was an email from Felicity. *Can't sleep. Knew you'd be up. GMT and all. I visited the White House Rose Garden on arrival. The White House. Wow. I can see myself standing there for the August summer picture. Top-tier interns get to stand in the top row. I'll be there.*

Top tier was for suck-ups. My anger at my twin steamed from my toes to my hair. We'd planned to refuse these internships. One in London. One in D.C. Refuse. Not go. Instead, she'd snagged the American internship and sent me overseas. And she assumed she'd beaten me like always. Shoved it in my face.

Britain probably didn't even have the same competitive rules as an American internship. For photos, they probably sorted everyone by family name. Names mattered here. Names and class. I'd be nicely in the middle. I locked my phone without replying and turned to the guy beside me.

He was one of those weird European contradictions.

Pressed clothes, shiny shoes, un-showered body. Yep, greasy flat hair. Shower every day for work, dude. Every day. What was so hard about that? This wasn't camping. "What'd I miss? Discussions on the weather? Soccer?"

"Nothing that wasn't in the packet." He turned more fully toward me, and his gaze took on a gleam of interest as he checked out my legs. "We're having a break before the Prime Family comes in." His tongue snaked out of his mouth to serve as his lip balm, allowing a glimpse of his teeth. Geez. No tooth brushing either?

"None of the assignments have been handed out, have they?" My sister's words dug at me. "It's not competitive, is it? Like who sits where for the group picture?"

"Interns with three points are top interns. They get to be in the group photo." His gaze dropped to my legs again, and he rubbed his hand along his own calf.

That made me nervous. Not his leg-rubbing, but the fact that they were limiting who would be in the photo. I needed to be in that photo. I shifted away and thumbed through my phone, searching for an explanatory email. There. I scrolled through the text.

Top interns were interns with three points. The all-important intern picture, the famous end of summer picture—the photo that would end up on my parents' mantle for the rest of my life.

Forever.

No doubt the image would make the rounds on our Christmas card, too. Tainting Christmas. My hand tightened on my teal phone case and grew clammy. I had to be in it.

My sister had forced me here; now she'd show me up. I

rubbed my temple with my free hand. Breathe. No, she wouldn't. Breathe.

One. Two. Three. Four.

Felicity in a photo on the top row, taken in the D.C. Rose Garden. Me, standing on wet London grass.

Felicity preening from the top row. Me, behind a hedge.

On the mantle.

Forever.

Or me, not in the photo at all. My pulse rose, and my intentions hardened. I could do this. I sat up straighter and read more from the email. No fraternization with the co-workers. Not a surprise. But it struck me just the same. No fraternization with Wythe. All summer. None. No touching. No...

The microphone whistled, drawing me out of my head.

Peppa stood on the small raised stage in front of us.

I swung forward with a new fervor for my internship. I'd nail my assignment. I had to.

Peppa adjusted the mic and centered her computer tablet on top of the wooden structure. "Now that the welcome is over, I'm in charge of handing out your summer jobs." Peppa clicked on her laptop, and an image of eggs lying in grass appeared on the screen behind her. "This live Internet status chart shows how effective you are at assisting Her Majesty's government." Peppa tapped on her computer.

A set of bleachers appeared. There were egg-shaped cartoon people on the yard in front of them. A cartoon egg rolled over to the platform and hopped up several bleacher rows until it was positioned below the top. "As head intern, last year I stood here beneath the Prime Family." Pride rounded her vowels. "Maybe you'll get the chance to stand beside me this year as the family celebrates their new term." Eggs dutifully filled in the bleacher.

A few suck-ups clapped.

Some eggs remained on the ground.

Peppa nodded in acknowledgment of her superior standing. "As you can see, there is not room for everyone. We reward successful effort." She held up her hands. "Now. It is my privilege—nay, my honor—to introduce the Prime Minister and her family. Please welcome the Prime Minister of the United Kingdom of Great Britain and Northern Ireland, the Right Honorable Vanessa Wise, of Her Majesty's Government."

The middle-aged blonde woman, the one I'd seen at the door to the breakfast room, came in, followed by a middle-aged man with graying, dark blond hair. Both wore suits and practiced, political smiles. I should have known what the Prime Minister looked like.

Everyone clapped.

I had known her name was Vanessa Wise and that her husband's name was Tom Wise. At least, I think I had known that. Okay, I hadn't. I had thought his name was David.

A small girl trotted out next. About six years old, she wore a pink dress with a blue satin ribbon tied at the waist.

"Her daughter, Caroline."

The intern on my left murmured, "Ahh. So precious."

"And their son, Wythe."

Wythe?

Chapter 4

My head shot up. That got me.

The hot blond guy from the closet and the scone buffet strode across the stage.

Wythe was not an intern. He wore a sure, confident expression. He waved at the crowd and moved into place with his family. Their positioning seemed well practiced. Everyone was in perfect view; no one blocked the other.

The blonde lady on my other side clutched her purse to her chest. Her gaze never left them.

My gaze flew back to Wythe.

Liar, liar, British pants on fire.

I should have done my research. Heat ran under my skin. No. He knew I thought he was another intern. He should have said something. Hot guys with hidden secrets. They were the worst kind of guys. And the best kind. My insides fluttered, and my weakness surprised me. I was so going to find him after this.

No. No, I wouldn't. There was a no-touching rule. I could look though, and I did.

I wasn't the only one who appreciated the sight of him. The women in the audience mumbled pleased yet restrained noises. So upper class. Enthusiasm was so middle class.

This hadn't been my morning. For an intriguing moment in the closet, it had been... Where had my mind gone? I think I'd already paired us up for the summer. Because of one unzipped dress and a scone.

Now he was on the other side of the line. A member of the family.

A family of four. Two kids. I swear, I thought there were three. Maybe the other one was the baby in diapers. Standing together, they formed a perfect family, posed with the lights glinting on their blond heads like halos. Ha. No one in politics wore a halo.

Two professional photographers squatted at the base of the stage to capture the moment. Wythe had gotten his build and square jaw from his father and his cut cheekbones from his mom. His eyes were all his own.

After a moment for pictures, the Prime Minister got behind the microphone and grinned at us. Her open palms and relaxed posture showed her welcome and appreciation. "Thank you for your service."

The Prime Minister motioned, and her husband stepped forward. He placed his hand on his wife's back, fully supportive, and leaned toward the microphone. "Your help over the summer will be invaluable to us, and it is our genuine hope it has some value to you."

Wythe stepped up next. "Thank you." His voice was deep, but it lacked the warmth he had used when he'd spoken to me directly.

Caroline walked forward and patted the side of his leg

with one hand. Wythe bent and lifted his adorable sister with one arm, high so she could reach the microphone. She beamed a dimpled smile at us and leaned forward. "Thank you, everyone." The microphone amplified her high, endearing voice.

They were a gorgeous family.

The crowd laughed and clapped. "Well done," the guy beside me said.

Commentary on the family filled the room. "So cute. So charismatic."

I saw it, too. One hour in, and I was already leaning in favor of the scone. Who knew what working here all summer with these charmers would do for my take on Britain? Maybe my annual three-week-long trips to the grandparents' Midlands farm hadn't shown me all that Britain could be. Maybe I'd discover more over these next six weeks.

I joined the clappers until the Prime Family exited from view.

Peppa retook the microphone. "Now for your placements. Take these and go through the main door to meet your groups and proceed with your team meetings." She ran through names, in no order I could discern. It wasn't alphabetical and only somewhat by category: public relations, security, business development… Maybe the order was by arrival, because by the time she got to my name, there was only me and a slim lady with beautiful dark blonde hair remaining in the audience.

I envied her hair. Loose curls a mix of dark and light, contained, perfect outfit, slim wristwatch. She hadn't been late. Beside her, I must've really looked a mess. She joined me in the first row. Her hands were clenched in her lap, and she breathed rapidly. Like hyperventilation rapid. Like get a paper bag or call the paramedic rapid.

At least I could breathe. In. Out. Yep. I was high functioning. Breathing and thinking. I'd throw in some talking. "You okay?"

"Yes," she squeaked. "I wonder where Zane was." Her voice sounded American Southern but less twangy than mine. Not East Coast Southern. Texas, maybe, but not my part. Her robin's egg blue gaze darted to me.

"No clue." I didn't know who Zane was. He must've been the third kid. I'd been right. I felt some satisfaction at that, since my being right hadn't happened much this morning.

"Georgiana Harper," Peppa said, her voice booming through the mic for an audience of two.

Georgiana, beside me, popped up. "That's me. I mean, call me Georgiana. I have my confidentiality agreement ready."

That reminded me to dig mine out.

Peppa clicked on the tablet and *Household* appeared on the screen behind her, though now there were only three of us in the room. She could have just said it. Peppa arched her eyebrows and her lips curved down.

Georgiana breathed faster, and her eyes grew glassy. "I'd hoped. I mean, I was counting, and I didn't think all the slots had been filled." Her gaze flew to me, and her breath broke. "Both guys are so gorgeous, and I'll be working for them."

"Yeah, sure." If thoughts of toting Wythe's laundry had her this unsteady, the poor girl wouldn't survive the week. And if the women in this country responded to Wythe with this kind of passion, his ego must've been deeper than the Atlantic. That was not a plus.

A picture of Caroline appeared beside Georgiana's name. "Oh, okay. I can help watch Miss Caroline." She squared her shoulders. "They live in the same house, you know. I will get to meet the guys. The whole perfect family. See them interact." The screen changed, showing her goals. "Get three frame-worthy photos of Ms. Caroline at charity events. I can do that." She smiled at me.

I smiled back. Georgiana was out of breath and overeager, but I liked her anyway. Peppa, not so much. How did I know who I'd like so quickly and who I'd dislike? Shouldn't I give Peppa more of a shot? I certainly needed a second shot after this morning's epic display of lateness. I'd make more of an effort.

More effort would hopefully mean more success. I'd match my sister's efforts and win a shot in the photo, like she would. I wished I had doubts about that, but a lifetime of competition let me know my sister would be on top. We were fraternal twins. I knew her. Now my head was in the game. I knew what mattered this summer.

Georgiana rose on her toes. "Charity events. The whole family could be there." She flushed. "I *will* get to meet Zane *in person*. Zane must be studying now. That's why he's not here. Both the sons. Engineers. Masters programs. So clever."

Yeah. Wythe had managed my tangled shirt and zipper. I could see the engineer in him.

Georgiana went up and exchanged paperwork with Peppa.

Feeling stupid, sitting there in the empty auditorium awaiting my fate, didn't work for me. I was the last one. I had to be next. I strode up on stage and joined the duo.

Peppa ignored Georgiana's chatter and smiled dismissively at her enthusiasm.

Georgiana's fervor made the confidentiality agreements we'd had to sign make even more sense. Basically, if I breathed a word of my summer to the press or in a tell-all book, I'd owe the British government a debt that would at minimum bankrupt me and at maximum involve me handing over my first-born child, along with the top half of my right foot. Or maybe it was that my future children would not be eligible for this program or something like that. The other rules weren't as harsh. But if I broke them, I'd be kicked out. I'd never live that down, so I'd never let that happen.

Georgiana must not have read the bolded "no talk, no touch" rule in the email. Or she wouldn't have been quite so excited to meet the Prime Brothers. Interns couldn't date anyone who worked or lived at Downing Street. Working here meant she and Zane wouldn't be holding hands over a lukewarm milkshake. Not this summer, anyway.

Holding onto the form, Peppa clicked the tablet and my name, Kira Kitman, and my super attractive passport photo appeared on the screen. The screen flickered.

A picture of Wythe appeared. My stupid heart jumped.

"Wythe." Georgiana stared at me with envy-glossed light-blue eyes.

I shrugged. But inside, there were happy tingles, and I know my mouth curved up. Wythe *could* hand-feed me scones each morning. *Welcome to Britain.*

Peppa frowned. She turned back to her tablet, muttered, and tapped on the screen. "That's a mistake. Someone erred. You are *not* with Wythe."

Again with using his name. I hated the sound of his name on her lips.

The next screen popped up. It listed my goals. *Wythe must attend three charity events this summer.*

Georgiana flushed a dark pink. Peppa paled.

"Looks like I am with Wythe," I said to dig the knife in. A skill honed by having a competitive sister. Plus, I wanted to say his name.

Peppa blew out a breath. "I did not assign you to Wythe. That is not correct. Someone is about to be on the hot seat." She threw her shoulders back and her chest out. "That phrase originated here, you know, because of the coals under the night watchman's chair."

A little less jetlag and a little less Peppa and I could appreciate that fact. But something about her didn't make me want to toss back a tequila shot and yell for more trivia.

Peppa made a snort-huff sound when I didn't respond quickly enough. "Shall we go get your real assignment sorted? I did not assign you to Wythe."

Repeating it wasn't going to change things. Peppa wasn't as in charge as she thought. I clung to that happy thought, but a twinge of annoyance made me roll my shoulders. *Get out of my business, Peppa.*

Maybe my annoyance this morning hadn't been hunger. My opinion was now cemented. I did not like Peppa. How did I know that already? Wisdom honed from childhood? Probably that. Peppa wore some micro-expression that I'd learned about during kindergarten. Maybe Felicity had worn it when she'd outrun me to the highest swing on the swing set, leaving me with the lower one.

"Come along, you two. The family lives upstairs."

"Upstairs." Georgiana breathed a low whooshing breath and fell into step. "We are close to them."

The family. Wythe. Yeah. Let's go there. I followed. "Shall we have a look behind the curtain?"

Chapter 5

Prime ministers' portraits hung along the stairwell wall in chronological order, marking decades of minute fashion changes: a narrower tie here, a wider lapel there, and one daring striped suit.

We ascended the marble, carpet-lined steps, and Georgiana muttered details about the leaders who caught her eye until we reached the portrait of Prime Minister Wise.

Georgiana flushed, which seemed to be her thing. She had that skin that didn't tan. I was fair, but my skin took on a Texas tan in the summer. Not this summer though. I'd be as snow-pale as her by August. Georgiana said, "They're perfect." Her voice was soft.

"No family's perfect." She'd know that if she had a sister like mine.

She didn't argue with me—just clasped her hands together and continued up the stairs. We went up one more flight to the third floor.

I showed my ID badge to the two guards protecting the private quarters. They checked Peppa's and Georgiana's, too.

Peppa pointed to the paneled door. "You two go in and make yourselves useful but unobtrusive. I'll get the assignments sorted." She continued down the hall.

Georgiana waved both hands in front of her face and stopped.

Inside, the Prime Family stood amid strategically placed couches and potted plants. Wythe sat in a blue overstuffed armchair, which was large enough that I could have curled up in it perfectly—me and a book. My unicorn shapeshifter erotica book. Me and him and my novel. There was a dream. Was he looking at me? He was.

No touching.

Georgiana muffled a moan.

"No family's perfect," I said again and gave Georgiana an encouraging look.

Georgiana wobbled on her heels. "The Wise family really is perfect. I don't have siblings. They are so lucky. Such a perfect unit. And we get to meet them."

"Breathe." I gave her a pat on the shoulder and then pushed her through the doorway.

Inside, the Prime Minister had her arms folded over her chest and was staring at her son and daughter as if she could will them into doing her bidding like she did Parliament.

"It's not happening," Wythe said without looking up from his computer tablet, firm dispassion in his voice.

We'd interrupted something. Georgiana paused. I kept walking.

"It's like the Salvador duck incident all over again. I won't have it. Mind your obligations." The Prime Minister took a step toward him and was blocked by her daughter.

Caroline, the six-year-old, cut in front of her and spun in a circle, chanting, "Never. Never."

I rather admired Caroline sticking to her position. If I'd done that more with my sister, maybe I wouldn't have been stuck with so many second choices.

A woman who knew about choices herself, the Prime Minister rubbed her temples like a mom at a grocery store. Her gaze flicked to us. "The handlers are here. Let them take over. I'll be in my office. I have a country to run." On that dramatic note, she delegated the problem to us and left.

Caroline tilted her chin in the air and spun faster. "Never. Never. No dog show." Her angelic public persona spun away with each twirl, and her blue eyes took on a wild light like her brother's. Wythe had probably started out with coal-matte eyes, and then his parents' demands had spun them into diamond brightness.

Despite her previous eagerness, Georgiana didn't go to Wythe. She knelt in front of the child. "I'm Georgiana, and I can take you to the Summer Kennel Club, where 2,500 champion dogs will compete. Proud stately breeds will vie for best in show." Georgiana had an unhealthy knowledge of dog trivia. Or she'd done her homework with the packet.

I'd enjoy learning some dog trivia. Was Trapper missing me? I knew he would when Felicity scooped out his wet food. She never gave him an extra scoop like I did. *Eat your dry kibble if you're still hungry,* she'd say. Trapper preferred the wet, smelly stuff. Because Felicity had stayed in the US, and interns there didn't live in the White House, she'd gotten to take Trapper with her. Jealousy streamed through me.

"You talk funny," Caroline said.

That was delightful. I was expecting a summer full of those type of comments.

"Caroline." Wythe's voice held caution and amusement. He still didn't look up from his tablet.

"You're an American, aren't you?" Caroline drew out the nationality as if it had even more syllables than four.

Wythe lifted his head and looked at me. "Now, Caroline. Manners."

Manners? How was that rude? *Proud to be an American here.* I moved to Georgiana's side. Something about the child's stance and attitude reminded me of my sister. I could take her. I had a lifetime of knowledge if I applied it correctly. I faced Georgiana, ignored Caroline, and said loudly, "I'll take Caroline's place. I hear there are real freaky-looking dogs there. Fluffy ones, baby ones."

"I want to see the baby dogs." Caroline's childish soprano pierced the air. Baby dogs in Scotland could have heard her clearly and were probably yipping right now. Caroline moved over to the large fireplace and stared at the mantle. A sleek, black, pointy-eared dog figurine hunched there by three cinnamon candles. She eyed the figurine with an intensity I'd only seen out of Trapper when I held a ball in front of him. "Freaky-looking dogs, too."

Georgiana glanced at me and then Wythe. "Should I get that down for her?"

"Yes," Caroline said in a hushed whisper, her gaze eager.

"It was a gift from the Egyptian ambassador," Wythe said.

Georgiana backed away. "Oh."

Caroline made a demanding sound, not a growl exactly, but close.

"Caroline…" Wythe said.

Caroline flushed and tore her gaze away. "I'm only looking at it." Each word was emphasized and defensive. They'd played this game before.

Georgiana held out her hand to Caroline, displaying her French manicure. "Why don't we find Nanny and look up puppy pictures? See if the Kennel Club's show is somewhere you'd like to go?"

"Nanny," Caroline squealed and ran from the room with Georgiana chasing after her.

That left me alone with Wythe. My palms prickled.

No touching.

Focus on the job.

Getting Wythe to the dog show would tick one charity event off my list. They'd set the bar too low for me. *Look at me go.* I moved closer. "How about you? You up for the dog show?" I sounded cool, like I was good with it either way. I'd concealed my hand. Wythe couldn't read me, so he had no advantage here. I also suspected he was as intrigued by me as I was by him. I'd read it in his expression. I had this.

"You show up late to scavenge the buffet and then think you can come in and *handle* me? I won't be as easily managed as my little sister," Wythe said without looking up.

He'd been a lot more charming when my dress had been undone. *A lot.*

Guys.

My cell beeped. Friends shouting out their plans for the day. As if I could join them from this side of the ocean. Oh, and another text from Felicity on the East Coast. Yay. Felicity had typed, *Things could not be more amazing. Click on the link to my new ringtone, "My Country 'Tis of Thee."*

The patriotic melody mocked me—it was the same one they used for the British national anthem, "God Save the Queen."

Annoyance made me hit reply, and I tapped on the speaker icon. "Sounds terrific. Things are beyond perfect here. Everyone's so amazingly agreeable. You won't believe it. Will send my new ringtone later. 'London Calling' maybe, or 'Oh What a Beautiful Morning.'"

Wythe snorted. "Who are you texting?"

"Not your business." Yeah. That was the way to win him over. I sighed. "My sister's interning at the White House. Family tradition. It's how I got this job." I waved the phone. "I'm competing for top intern from across the pond." I made my voice sound enthused but still cool, showing none of my roiling anger or frank desperation.

Wythe looked me dead straight in the eyes.

My heart caught.

He shook his head. "Give it up. I did my duty during the campaign. Now that we're in office, they can soldier on without me. I won't have my family paraded about." He rounded his words in that posh educated way. His tone said his decision was final, but it just challenged me.

He didn't get to decide my fate. I would be in that intern picture. I'd get three points. I'd find a way to get him to those public events. A bribe maybe. I pretended to drop the subject.

"What are you reading?" I hoped his answer wouldn't be weird British porn. What'd that even look like? If American porn stars looked like Barbie dolls, and don't get me started on the creep factor there, what did the British ones look like? I guessed there were loads of buttons involved. However, I

41

had no plans to find out. He'd better answer carefully.

"Not your business." He imitated my words and Texas accent.

I was not charmed. A wave of tiredness hit me, and I couldn't think about how to work this situation. "I'm too jetlagged to deal with your porn habit. We'll talk about this tomorrow." I gave him a pointed look. My dark blue eyes didn't have the same brightness as his, but I could stir up intensity when I wanted to. "This is far from over."

His gaze had a hard edge, a hint of the matte-coal they used to be. "You lost before you got here. You just don't know it yet."

I should not have found his words or his expression hot, but I did. Heat rose from my neck to my face. My chest lifted and fell faster. Maybe I was just annoyed with him. That was it. I wanted to fling the tablet from his hands, but he had me beat by a good six inches in height and fifty pounds in weight. Crap, they measured using the metric system. I'd have to start converting in my head. He had twenty-two kilograms on me and...wait, no, they used stones. He had four stones on me, and...forget it. Jetlag made conversions difficult. Just thinking of the flight over made the haze of sleepiness hit me. I drummed my fingers against my skirt and turned to walk out. "Tomorrow." I said it like a promise, but it came out husky, kind of sexy, as if my voice knew of my subconscious desires and was offering them up to him.

He shifted in the chair behind me, and I resisted looking back. If I looked back, he'd know he had me.

When I got to the doorway, two security guards in dark suits rushed past. One held his hand straight up and tapped his fingertips into the palm of his other hand. "Move, move, move."

I stepped aside, and my heartbeat picked up, pacing itself double-time, skipping past all the stopped beats Wythe had caused. I scanned the room to figure out what was going on. Nothing. I saw nothing. No smoke. No fire. No hail of bullets.

Wythe rose and sighed. Not perturbed at all.

Whereas my wild jump had woke me right up.

The first guard grabbed Wythe's arm and led him toward the door in a fast clip.

The other guard spun back and scanned the surroundings. "Clear." He pulled the arm on his headset until the microphone rested in front of his mouth. "We have Turnstile. Repeat."

Confusion tangled my mind. Logic said, *hang back*. Logic said, *I don't know these people or this situation*. Something illogical moved me to go to Wythe for reassurance. "What's going on?"

Wythe snagged my arm and pulled me into the group, now headed out the door.

The lead guy started to run.

Chapter 6

Wythe kept hold of my arm, as if I'd leave. "Threats and drills are treated the same." His British voice came out educated and crisp. "I'm sure you read the packet." His fingers tightened, and I half-jogged to keep up. My ballet flats thumped on the floor. I needed running shoes.

Darn packet. No, I hadn't read the packet. What was going on?

We passed Georgiana, standing in a doorway, her mouth agape.

Other members of the household seemed to be carrying on as if nothing was happening. A maid folding towels. A footman dusting a giant globe. We turned off the main hallway and down a narrower corridor. No pictures on the wall, no carpet runner on the worn tile floor.

"I read some of the packet." *None of it.* Well, I'd read page one. "Threat?" Adrenaline rushed through me, shoving away all the jetlag. "Where are we going?" I glanced at the lead guy and kept pace with their slow trot. What had seemed like running now felt really slow. My heart was thumping faster than our steps. "Point me the way. I can run way faster than this. Way faster." I wasn't proud of the shrillness in my voice, but I wasn't ashamed either. This was like in grade school, when an alarm had gone off and we'd all done this slow unrealistic trot outside to line up. Had there been a real emergency, we would've run like crazy. That's what we should have practiced, a realistic wild run and a slide to hit the dirt. Why? Why were we trotting? Was this somehow more civilized? Alarms weren't meant to be civilized. They were…

Wythe tightened his grip on my arm like he sensed that I'd bolt into the wall. I might.

"Keep in step," the lead said, his head swiveling, assessing the passageway. He opened a side door and led us down flights and flights of stairs.

Gravity sped us up, but not enough, and my anxiety rose at their methodical plod, which was more suited to the tenth lap on the jogging track in Texas heat than a Downing Street emergency. *Tell them to sprint. Make them get it.* My mouth opened, and I sucked in a breath. I pushed on the navy-suited guard in front of me. "Move. Faster."

He didn't.

Wythe shook my arm, so I'd focus on him. "They have to clear the area before we move."

That was actually good thinking, and his even tones helped reassure me. "Got it. Clear that passage." My voice came out loud, over-loud.

Wythe winced. "We should keep quiet, you know. Not tip off the non-existent threat."

"Oh. Right." I shut up. Non-existent. That had to be good, right?

At the bottom, we came up against a long hall and a steel door with no knob. The guard typed in a key code on a security pad. Wythe pressed his face close to the panel for an ocular scan, and the door slid open.

I bounced on the balls of my feet, searching the stretch for anything out of the ordinary. "Really? An eye scan, that's the fastest way to secure us?"

Wythe yanked me through the entrance. The door shut and clanked with a lock, sealing us into a dark room, alone together.

The hairs on my arms rose, and I blinked to adjust to the lack of light. "What just happened?" My voice came out in a whisper. Not a sexy, me-and-him-in-the-dark kind of whisper, but a strained one.

"Room's soundproofed. You can speak up." Wythe sounded bored.

I tried to steady my nerves and failed. My shoulders folded in, and I wrapped my arms around myself. "I get the stiff upper lip thing, I even admire it, but my American lips are quivering. Aren't you concerned?"

I couldn't see Wythe. How was he so calm? Was he calm? Was he lying? I felt for his wrist to check his pulse. It was slightly fast under my fingers, nothing like the way mine raced. He said nothing.

"It could be anything. Bomb. Shooter." Panic escalated in my voice. I threw out my arm to feel for a wall or one of their hidden doorknobs. "Will they get Georgiana? Caroline? Your mom?"

"Shh," Wythe said. "They're fine. We're fine. You're safe. The emergency lights will kick on in a second. I've been in this panic room before. There's plenty of space and supplies."

46

"What if one of the guards is a bad guy and they trapped us down here?"

"It was a drill."

"But how do you know?"

"Sit." He pulled me to the floor and took hold of my forearms.

The concrete was hard and cold but solid beneath me. Supportive.

"Breathe. Breathe with my count. In. One. Two. Three. Out. One. Two. Three. Four. Five. Six." His voice sounded deep and strong in the dark and unafraid. He clearly believed this was a drill. "In. Out." He kept the inhales half the length of the exhales.

My breathing slowed, and my heart rate calmed under his instructions. My senses other than survival kicked in. I was close enough to breathe in his cologne, a kind of posh guy sophisticated cologne. I wanted to crawl forward and breathe in deeper. My shoulders eased, and his fingers moved in soothing circles on my inner arms. He traced large figure-eights from my elbow to my wrist. Infinity. He was tracing infinity into my arms. The motion was addictive. I curled my nails into my palms.

More.

In my romantic popular fiction class, the professor played a Romance Writers of America workshop recording. The author had lectured on putting sex in the middle of a stressful situation. She'd called it, "stop, drop, and roll." I'd thought that was a crazy trope. Now I got it. Everything in me was heightened, falling apart, and Wythe anchored me. I could see grabbing ahold of him.

"They run drills all the time. We react as if the threat's real."

My brain had fuzzed out, but I forced myself to concentrate on his words. "You don't think this is real?" My voice came out calm and steady, making me proud.

His warm hands dropped away, and I missed them instantly. "I refused to do my duty and attend the kennel show. Mother called a drill. A little reminder of my obligations."

This was over the dog show. No way. They'd scared the hell out of me because he'd refused to go to the dog show. I sucked in a breath, losing my calm rhythm. It was like one of my sister's manipulations times ten. "What?" Shock colored my voice, outrage replaced my fear, and I slapped the concrete floor with my palms. "You don't want to go to the dog show, so they throw you in a dark closet?" My hands were waving in the air now, though he couldn't see them.

"Nothing so Harry Potter."

It wasn't funny.

He half-laughed. "They'll secure the area, get an all-clear, and we'll be out in fifteen. I don't have to live down here hiding my magic."

I liked his turns of phrase, and I wanted to be distracted. "What magic?"

This time, he full-on chuckled and tugged on a strand of my hair. "The longest I've stayed in a panic room has been an hour, and that was during a storm with com problems."

I wanted to lean into his hand or have him thread his fingers in my hair. He didn't. "Storm? Like rain? Because rain is all you've got here. Why didn't they build a rain-proof bunker? Don't they live here? Don't they know? We'll be stuck here for hours." I wasn't proud of the escalation of my tone, but I wasn't ashamed of it either. My emotions were fluctuating like a carousel of books at the library, a fast one where the books tumbled off. "Hours." My eyes had adjusted. I couldn't really see him but knew from my other senses that he sat crisscross in front of me while my legs curled to the side because of my dress. Dresses were no good in emergencies. I grabbed his knees.

"I don't hate it." His voice deepened.

As if timed, the overhead fluorescent lights buzzed on.

The light calmed me down in a different way than his breathing exercise. We'd be fine. We were in a bunker. The room held a shelf of supplies, food, computer equipment, and bedding. A couch squatted against the far wall by an interior door. Bunkers meant stir crazy, cabin fever, and escalating paranoia. But we were safe.

We needed out.

Wythe rose, pulling me up with him and over to the couch.

I was in no mood to stop, drop, and roll. Those books had it wrong. I dusted my palms off on my thighs and sat on the overstuffed cushion, ready to run again, but the couch didn't let me keep my coiled posture. The couch had lost its support decades ago and sucked me in. My skirt slid up my thighs. I tugged it down.

Despite the bunker's age and secrecy, the room had been cleaned recently. The air smelled of apple polish, like the foyer and the furniture at my grandparents' house. Must've been a British brand. At home, cleansers were more lemon or orange-scented. Apple didn't scream clean. Our country had started with British immigrants. Maybe that's where we got our fondness for apple pie, some urge for the fragrances from our homeland.

Wythe eyed me with his impossibly blue eyes, in the way the European men did. American men stared at girls, too, but they were less obvious about it. I caught his gaze. His eyes were fascinating, like gemstones. I could look into his bright eyes a long time.

I leaned my head into the couch cushion and did just that.

He arched his eyebrows. "What made you choose to do this with your summer?" His tone was neutral, but I could tell my decision hadn't impressed him.

I blinked. Confessing that my sister tricked me into it sounded lame.

I shrugged.

He looked away.

It made me feel lost for a moment. Like I'd had a chance to connect with him. And I'd missed it. It was one of those moments I didn't know how to get back.

The door clanked and swung inward.

Wythe rose to his full height with an athletic fluidity.

I scrambled up beside him, heart re-thumping, head re-spinning, new nausea forming. "What do we do? It could be anyone coming in. Where are the weapons?"

"Protocol..." Wythe began to answer.

A guard peered in. "All clear." He assessed me with cautious eyes set deep in his serious face.

Adrenalin left me with his words. "Thanks." As all the high-caution chemical reactions left my body, my lack of sleep fought with a new shaky feeling. My stomach squished. I felt sick, physically sick. "I've got to go. Can you point me to room 5B?" That or Heathrow Airport. This place was crazy.

The guard pointed and held his arm out for me to precede him.

I turned to look back at Wythe, who was watching me quietly. I didn't know what to say, and I didn't want to thank him for the comfort while we were standing in front of the guard. I settled on a small nod.

He returned it.

A very British exchange.

"Okay, then."

"I'm going to find my brother and go for a run." His voice was tight, but his eyes were on me, a lingering hint of concern in them. "See you tomorrow?"

I nodded. Where did he run? Outside? In a gym? That was a good way to burn off his adrenaline. I'd go watch. No. I was wiped out. I had to snap out of this or I'd lose myself on day one. I struggled to give him an American thumbs-up instead.

I went up to the top floor, again, no elevator, and the guard pointed down the hallway. "Intern and staff apartments are on this floor." I waved and walked down the corridor to 5B, breathing deeply through my nose and closing the world out.

Concentrate on the mundane. Get out of your head.

The apartment was better and worse than I'd expected. In terms of décor, it had the same old-building, tall-ceiling, crown-molding vibe that the rest of the place did. A studio apartment. Probably 300 square feet. A two-seater sofa, a TV on a chest of drawers, and a partial kitchenette with a mini-fridge and a microwave. I shuddered to think what rent on this tiny place would draw, given its central London location. Maybe 2,000 pounds per month. That was about 3,000 dollars, or 4,000, depending on the conversion rate.

In Texas, that would get me a four-bedroom house on the right side of town or a whole semester in the dorm.

In September, when I wrote my first rent check, I'd laugh at the memory of this place. Assuming I got a job. Lit degree, new graduate for hire didn't scream "Compete for me" to most corporations. Finishing this program would do more than keep me even with my sister. It would give me an edge in the job market, one that my choice of major didn't provide.

I pushed through the tiredness, knowing I needed to scope out the room because if I stopped moving, I'd collapse right there. *Bed, where are you?*

The total square footage was small, but I liked the privacy more than I liked the idea of more space or a commute. A corner door opened into a small bathroom. A twin bed lay under the slanted roof, and an armoire served as a closet. Both were weird. We didn't build rooms like this in Texas. No one had anything but a flat ceiling; no one I knew anyway. I was a tall American servant in a British period drama with no interest in serving.

Someone had placed my bags in here. I thought about showering and unpacking, but the tsunami of tiredness was taking me down. I put my bag in front of the door to trap invaders and traded my dress for a t-shirt. I probably had somewhere to be, but the jetlag wouldn't let me care.

I grabbed my book and crawled onto the hard, twin mattress. I knew I should read my informational orientation packet...but I didn't. The book I was reading was not recommended in any of my literature classes. However, I knew it would truly take me out of my own head. *Hornicorn: An Erotic Shape-Shifting Unicorn Paranormal* was the kind of reading material that did that. I turned the page.

Aurelia-corn pranced through the forest until she reached the reflecting pool. She looked down upon her unicorn image and thought of her lost love. Longing and lust rolled through her. "Oh, Brady-corn. When? When will you return to me?"

She thought of their time in the waterfall, and then again in the rose fields. Afterward, he'd made her a wreath of petal pink roses. And when she sniffed it. Ah, when she sniffed it, the memories rolled through her like the most potent lustrous lust dust.

She knew where he was. The evergreen forest. But she could not go there. Not yet. Not until she could fully open her heart again and offer him her hoof.

Rain pattered against my window. The book folded over my hand. I'd close my eyes a moment…

When I woke up, soft London light from the window told me it was afternoon. I rolled out of bed and checked my cell phone. The screen read *low battery* and 18:30 or *6:30 PM*. Great. I was wide awake now as if I had the whole evening ahead of me. A day I'd already lived.

Ugh, I'd done what everyone advised against after an overseas flight. I'd gone to sleep. I unpacked, plugged a converter into the wall jack, and plugged my phone in. A pop sounded, and smoke puffed out. Ignoring the slight burning smell, I pulled out the electrical converter and just used the plug part. Smartphones weren't supposed to need electrical converters anyway. I crossed my fingers and found another wall outlet.

I needed to read my packet. I didn't want to. I wanted a cup of English Breakfast tea. One dose of caffeine and I'd be thinking clearly. I leaned into the counter and stared at the kettle. *Go steam, go.*

My phone buzzed. The video chat came on. Felicity was on the floor doing sit-ups in front of a small two-seater dining table. Her accommodations weren't much bigger than mine if she only had that small table. But at least she had a table. "Did you get all my texts? You didn't respond to them all." She said the sentences between sitting up.

"Must be the Wi-Fi here." She actually might believe that, given the sketchy Wi-Fi at our grandparents' house. But probably not. London had killer Wi-Fi.

Trapper barked through the speaker. Longing, homesickness, and envy stirred in my belly. Trapper, our black and white Japanese Chin, crawled around the table legs, looking for crumbs. I knew he'd find some. Trapper had mad crumb-hunting skills.

Then it hit me again. Anger. I wanted Trapper here with me. I propped the phone on the counter and moved away so Felicity wouldn't see she'd gotten to me. I poured the hot water over the teabag. Steam wafted the tea fragrance into the room. *Calm down. Calm down. Don't let her see your reaction.*

"Did it arrive?" Felicity asked.

I blanked my expression and moved back into view while glancing across the counter. A fat over-stuffed package sat there. Return address. *White House. Felicity Kitman.*

As if the post office in DC used the words *White House.* We both knew she lived off the grounds. She'd penned that to dig at me.

I tore open the end.

Chapter 7

I was not enthused about the gift. It was from Felicity, after all. A gray-green wool sweater bulged from the opening, trying to escape. Threads of resentment tightened in my chest. I couldn't breathe enough to form an answer, or a curse word, or a lie.

"It came today, didn't it? The package I sent you?" Felicity asked.

I lifted it from the box and held it in front of the camera lens, blocking my expression.

We'd both gotten wool sweaters for graduation. What Texan didn't want a wool sweater for graduation? Especially one made from Grandpa's own sheep. I had used my own graduation sweater for a cushion in Trapper's dog bed.

"There are ways to rainproof it." Felicity twisted her upper body so she faced the screen, her hands behind her head, her elbows out. "You'll need to Google that."

I shoved it back in the box, my fingernail snagging the wool. I shook free and grabbed my mug of tea. The hot wet drink spilled over the back of my fingers, burning. "Mmm, yes. So thoughtful. It is summer here, you know."

"Oh, I know." Felicity resumed her sit-ups. My sister had more discipline. It had gotten her a higher class rank, an attentive boyfriend, and longer nails, currently painted hot lavender. She'd doomed me in the womb to come in second like my birth order.

Trapper barked and slicked his pink tongue across a table leg. I didn't ask what had spilled. I didn't offer any further conversation, just toyed with my jagged thumbnail, picking at the tear and the snagged strand of wool. I needed a file.

Neither my sister nor I had wanted to be interns, but family pressure was a heavy thing. Dad had been a summer intern for the White House; Mom had been an intern for the Prime Minister. It was how our parents had met, at an international function in London.

Here's an opportunity on a silver platter. Take it.

We didn't want it. We'd agreed on saying no together. The intern family tradition would end with us. We'd gone into Dad's office. I'd chickened out and pushed Felicity forward. "Go ahead, Felicity, tell them what we decided."

Felicity had pointed at Dad's computer screen. "Is that the email to the president's coordinator?" She knew full well it was. Our parents pressured us about it daily.

"Yes." Dad squeezed lemon into his iced tea. "Well?"

"Type my name there." Felicity smiled big and tapped the screen. "I can't wait to see Old Glory flying over the capital."

I froze at the betrayal. We were supposed to be turning down these internships.

Mom clapped and then lightly patted my shoulder. "You chose England?" Her tone grew sentimental, and her British accent hit heights that needed subtitles. Twenty years in America and she hadn't lost it.

Panic, betrayal, and a grave dislike for the island that was Britain clogged my throat, but love for Mom muted me.

Dad tapped on the screen, shooting our acceptances across the states and over the pond. The clicking keyboard screamed in my ears like an amplified commercial.

Felicity leaned across the table. Victory glowed around her like the sparkle-dust on her cheeks. "I'll lend you my new wool sweater." She winked. "You're going to need it."

She'd made good on the promise. Here I was in England, clutching her sweater.

Felicity had been a total sneak then and was rubbing it in my nose now.

She was going down. I moved my mouth like I was talking. "…Wi-Fi…" I said and shut off the video chat. I'd make the most of my evening and then fit in some exercise of my own so I could possibly sleep tonight.

***

Sleep that night was fitful, but I was going to make the next day great. I was going to go see Wythe, but first I checked the rest of the apartment. I found unfrosted flakes in the kitchen, ate a handful, brushed my teeth, showered, and dressed. They'd given us the wireless Internet key code along with my physical room key, a heavy brass thing. Sitting cross-legged on the couch in jeans and a t-shirt, I logged in.

After checking my favorite Internet sites: email, movie news, and the university website, I checked the forum set up for the interns. When I clicked on my name, I got a further login that showed charity event options for the summer. I went back to the main screen and clicked on the giant green circle that said Intern Status. Fifty or so eggs lay in a pile. A few had rolled onto the grass. They were headed toward a set of bleachers. I was so going to be up high on those bleachers when we took that August intern photo.

Glorious blond bobble-headed images of the Prime family stood at the top of the bleachers. I'd need three points to be in that photo with them.

Why couldn't my parents have met at a bar?

I hovered the cursor over an egg. A name popped up along with a score. I clicked compulsively over the eggs until I found mine. As I clicked on it, a waft of green steam rose off the top. *Kira Kitman. Arrived late. Missed Chelsea flower show.*

Wait. The flower show was in May. I'd gotten points off because Wythe didn't show up at a flower show last week? The Royal Horticulture Society could… I let the thought die off. It wasn't their fault. The fault was Wythe's. He'd pay.

Right now.

I headed out, going down the stairwell a level to the main residences. Wythe's rooms were on the third door down on the right, per the guard. Peppa caught up with me at the top of the hall. "You missed the Chelsea Flower Show special summer exhibit."

I paused. "I saw that."

"It was today. I'm sure you saw that in the packet."

"Okay." I didn't elaborate further, since I'd already said that I'd seen it. Though I'd only seen it afterward. And not in the packet. I smiled a polite but distant smile, one of those that don't show teeth or show in my eyes, and moved down the hall.

Peppa paced me and held out a computer tablet. "Now might be a good time to go over Wythe's schedule." Peppa was on the petite side compared to me. If I wasn't going to ignore her, I'd have to slow my walking pace to match hers.

"Thanks." I took the tablet with a glance at Wythe's schedule. Pleasure and confusion swirled in me. It was odd that I wasn't assigned to some American contingency, but I wouldn't buck the assignment. A quick glance at Peppa showed me how annoyed she was, eyes narrowed, stance rigid. "So, this means…I'm assigned to Wythe, after all." I kept my words slow and dug in with a deeper Texas drawl than I possessed. Obviously, it meant that, and it meant Peppa didn't have the power to get me moved. Peppa needed that little reminder. *Search for easier prey.* Neither Peppa nor Felicity were stomping on me any further. Not this summer. Not ever.

Peppa tapped on the bright blue box in the corner as if I weren't moving fast enough for her. The calendar filled with tiny text and words like *cricket, derby,* and *garden.* "Charity options are listed here." She pointed to a tall door at the end of the hall, the same one the guard had already directed me to. "Go on in. It appears you are staying. For now." Her voice sounded tight. Her bottled rage would backfire one day. *Keep it on the inside.*

I had to admit I did want my assignment. Not just to stump her, but Wythe was…well, I didn't know what he was yet, but he did interest me. "Thanks," was all I said. I'm not one to draw out a gloat. That trait went to my sister. I preferred a milder celebration, a glowing, internal joy.

I continued down the yellow corridor, walking faster now, internally chanting the name of the first event to make it happen. *Dog show. Dog show. Dog show.*

Peppa paced me.

I did not need her watching me as I persuaded Wythe to attend the dog show. I got to his door and knocked.

No answer. I turned the knob. Were my hands sweaty? *Yes.* Were my insides eager? *Yes.*

"Don't go in yet." Peppa held up a hand and was still freaking watching me. "Wait. You should wait. That's Wythe's private study."

Waiting would not get him out in public. I stepped in, and Peppa followed me. A seating area consisted of a pair of wing-back chairs and end tables. Empty seats. A large desk, made of ornate rosewood, which couldn't be his style, centered between bookcases. Empty black executive-style chair. Picture window, gray English sunlight, window seat.

Wythe sat at one end, ignoring the garden and us and typing on his laptop. He wore dark trousers and a navy shirt. Not the usual casual at-home wear.

He typed, then paused and read, and then typed some more.

The sight of a guy hunched over his laptop made me flinch. I did not want to know what he was reading. My friends always thought they did and blithely popped over a guy's shoulder, but I'd seen that cause more than one breakup. Okay, it had caused one of mine, the last one. But I'd learned my lesson.

Peppa shifted on her feet, and her gaze moved, too, as if searching for a reason to stay. She was probably going to come up with some boss-type excuse to observe my work.

I had to shut that creepy idea down before she got the idea and dug her sensible shoes into the rectangular rug with the unfortunate floral pattern. I raised my eyebrows at her like *What do you need?*

Her gaze was on Wythe.

He still hadn't looked up, but he'd stopped typing. His posture had that kind of alert motionlessness that said he knew he was being watched but was choosing to ignore us.

That seemed to do it for Peppa. She turned and left, leaving the door open.

I shut it and moved to stand by the window seat. The sun was up but clouds softened the light. I started with a comment on the décor. "You have a passion for daffodils and shamrocks, huh?"

He glanced at the rug. "Gift from the Irish ambassador."

I had my doubts but took his bothering to answer as an invitation. I climbed up with my back to the opposite wall, so I was facing him. The window seat was firm, covered in a rose print fabric, and not as plush as I'd want. It was the kind of thing that made me realize this place wasn't a real home. He'd have replaced the floral rug and this cushion. This was a furnished loaner home, a crazy expensive, historic loaner.

Kind of like me. I was a crazy, young, international loaner secretary.

Time to persuade.

I positioned myself cross-legged and leaned forward with my elbows on my knees. I had a great view of his polished leather loafers from here. Barely any scuff marks. Scuff marks must mean a lack of control, resulting in lower voter confidence. But really, who wore loafers while reading alone at home? He wanted to go out.

He wanted to go out to the dog show. Now, I had to make him realize that truth. By any means necessary, even honesty. "I have zero points on the intern status sheet. But I don't want to manipulate you into going to the dog show." I was being sincere despite my agenda. I widened my eyes and flipped my palms up in the universal, "nothing to hide" gesture.

Wythe looked up and eyed me steadily with his bright blue knowing gaze. "What's wrong with manipulation?"

Was he teasing me? Flirting? Challenging me? I couldn't read him.

"I'll be straight with you. I need you to go to the dog show so I can get an intern point." I put it all out there for him, being honest. Now it was his turn to respond.

He still held his computer. Was he busy? I'd just finished college, and it was hard to shake the feeling that I had deadlines, but I didn't. The pressures of college were over for me. Maybe that was his reason for resisting the event. "We don't have to stay for the whole champion breed winner selection. Just make an appearance. It'll be quick."

I gestured to his computer. "Are you finishing a class?" This was shaky ground, because I did not want to end up typing his term papers. What would that teach me? This internship was for me; I was supposed to be benefitting. In essence, he worked for me. He owed me the dog show as a way of sharing knowledge of his culture. Knowledge I'd return home with to America, enriched and ready for my real job. Whatever that would be.

"How do you know I'm not searching for someone to fancy me? An online love match?"

I ignored his sarcasm, tilted my head, and refrained from sharing my sordid theories as to his browsing history. "I'm prepared to make a straight-up offer for the favor." I put intrigue into my voice to tempt him.

His gaze was on my lips. "Let's hear it then."

What did I want to do for him? I eyed his perfectly

pressed clothes and monogrammed shirt. He didn't need a valet. I wasn't doing that. He'd mentioned online love, and he'd been looking at my mouth. Sometimes people made jokes about what they really wanted.

I checked out his mouth. Nice lips.

"Let's hear it," he repeated, his blue gaze even more intent on me, as if he were reading my mind and willing me to say it.

"A kiss," I said.

A kiss.

My brain went blank. Meant to think that, not say it.

Said it though.

How long had the room been quiet? My heart pumped faster, and heat flushed my lips. I waited for his response.

Wythe's grip on his laptop slipped. The screen tilted and slid. He caught the base before it fell and put it on the ledge beside him. "Okay then, I'd do that."

The sincerity in his voice was hot. I wanted to melt forward, lean into him, onto him. Flat out on him and kiss him right then.

I leaned away, back against the wall, instead.

Had I just creeped on him?

He worked for me.

Sort of.

Or I worked for him.

I tilted my head. He didn't look creeped out. That was the definition, right? How the other party took it. He looked extremely interested. This hot handsome guy was into me. I liked that. Though kissing did probably fall under the "no touching" rule. Maybe. Ah, well, what Peppa didn't know wouldn't destroy my summer.

A kiss.

His agreement had been fast. I should have offered to hold his hand and worked my way up from there. Live and learn. The bargain was struck.

His computer screen was now angled toward me.

I shouldn't look, but I couldn't not look.

I looked.

Chapter 8

Wythe's computer screen was split. One had numbers, some kind of math. The other screen had cryptic words. *Car park. Sun. Not new.*

Not what I'd expected. I'd expected sports, or loose women, or…I don't know, engineer stuff. Whatever that was. Equations.

Instead, it was cryptic. Like a puzzle. The clues popped answers into my brain: *Car park.* Parking lot. Like where the news had reported that they'd found their king. *Sun. Not new.* I knew the answer. I pointed at the laptop. "Richard the third. Mom says he got a bum rap, but I don't know." Okay, that was one thing I liked about Britain—the history and the literature. Austen. Bronte. Churchill.

Wythe froze and leaned back. "What's that?" A sharp tone entered his voice. He looked a little stunned.

I had it right. Didn't I? I re-read the onscreen words before I spoke again. *Car park. Sun. Not new.* "Richard the third. He made the news at home when y'all dug him up out of a parking lot. That was epic."

Wythe slid off the window seat and paced along the dark maroon rug covering the hardwood floors. "Richard the third." He clapped his hands together with one sharp pop. "I should have seen it." He returned and tilted the computer so we both could see the screen easily as he typed in the answer. *Correct* flashed across the screen, followed by red flashes. "This lit class sucks."

I was not offended. Not everyone could love literature... or even *Hornicorn*. Someone had to do math. "My degree's literature. You know. Richard III, Shakespeare. 'The sun of York. Made glorious summer of this sun of York; and all the clouds that lour'd upon our house.'"

His eyes glazed over and lost their feral brightness, so I stopped quoting Shakespeare.

My mouth curved, and I tried to squelch my amusement. Nor did everyone appreciate a fine turn of phrase. Maybe he'd like how I'd solved the puzzle part. "We don't say 'car park' in Texas, and Mom commented on the newscaster saying, 'parking lot.'" I shook my head. "I was young, but I remember it because it was such a cool story. Finding your king buried under a parking lot. Way to revere."

Wythe tapped on the computer, shooting off an email. "We're not allowed outside help on this project. I'll have to forfeit the answer and take the time penalty if I don't make you my partner. I'll send the professor your information." He said it as if it were decided, as if I'd agreed to something.

I was still recuperating from some jetlag, so I wasn't fully tracking. "Partner in what?"

"My final class is literature. I have to finish the class. There's a treasure hunt going. The more clues you solve, the higher your grade, and it drives you toward an answer to the ultimate class question. Get it wrong, and I'm stuck with a thousand papers."

And I could help him get it right, by taking the class with him. No. "I'm done with school. Graduated." Bachelor of Arts in Literature. *Check.* Real life job prospects. *Zero.* And frankly, my brain was a bit fried over it all. I needed the *Hornicorn* book to escape and clear my literary palate. No more classes for me. "Nope. I'm done."

"This is your love. Literature. Or so you implied." Wythe spoke like a lawyer at a serial killer murder trial. His expression was determined, unrelenting. He was manipulating me, and he wasn't going to accept a refusal.

I did love books. And this would give me bargaining power with him. Plus, I'd get time with this hot guy who intrigued me. I'd help him. I'd even join his class. But he didn't need to know that yet. "Why don't you have a class partner already?" Class partner. Life partner. I had many more questions for him. I should relax; I had six weeks to get to know him. But I had a desire to know about his personal life right now, and it was making me quiz him.

He shifted toward the window. The weak British sun glinted against his blond hair and bright eyes. The understated glow framed him like the subject of a painting, and it was almost too much for me. Wythe would've been unbearably handsome in the brightness of the Texas sun.

"I did have," Wythe said. "Vihaan Laghari. It didn't work out." He waved his hand like he was shooing away the rest of his evasive answer. "Vihaan jumped ship and became Peppa's partner."

"Peppa, as in…" I jerked my thumb toward the door because I didn't want to say, 'Head Intern Peppa' and I couldn't recall her last name. "And no one else would team up with you?" I didn't believe that at all.

He frowned. "None for the right reasons. I turned them down to go it alone. But I need someone to bounce ideas off. You'll do."

I'll do? How super not hot.

He clicked on a website, and navy blue filled the background along with an image of the honey-colored Oxford University.

I didn't know their admission requirements, but I knew I couldn't get in. That was an old-money, old-school, freak smart kind of place. Or maybe new money was let in, too, as long as the student had the freak smarts. I was reading a book called *Hornicorn*. Should I put that on my application and imagine the admissions letter getting tossed in the can? My eyebrows rose. "I can't get into Oxford." I couldn't even feel embarrassed about the statement. Oxford was that far out of my reach.

He waved me off. "My mother's prime minister. You'll get in."

There was that. A prime minister could get me a passport or a new identity. She could probably get me in to audit a class at Oxford. Wythe had me there. And, somehow, he'd taken over our meeting. Bargain, bargain, bargain. I had the one point with the dog show. I needed two more points. "I might do this. But you'll have to do an event for me, too."

"Of course. We've already agreed on that. The price is one kiss for the dog show."

"Didn't I just solve your puzzle? That won't get me the dog show? You want a kiss, too?" I was teasing him now, because I was totally open to the kiss and pretty much had been since he'd zipped me up in that dark closet.

"We already struck up an agreement. Gentlemen don't renege on their agreements."

I rather liked that, but I crossed my arms over my chest and tapped my shoe while tilting my face away in a classic hard-to-get pose.

He huffed out a breath. "Maybe. A second event. If you can solve the whole puzzle."

I could do that. I didn't stop my grin. "Tell me all you know."

"English Literature. The ultimate." He said the words flatly, as if he couldn't imagine anything worse.

That was the whole puzzle? *English Lit. The ultimate.* "That could be anything. The ultimate in not finding a job. Or the ultimate in alphabet use or…"

His mouth quirked up and his posture eased. "I didn't think you'd solve it so readily."

I might have. This was my degree, after all. If he'd given me more of a clue. "So now you get a kiss…and a classmate."

His gaze fell to my mouth. "There is that." His voice was deep and a little playful.

I really liked it. A lot. "I'm feeling outmaneuvered." I wasn't, and he knew I wasn't.

His expression was intent, and it melted me. *Talk to me more. Maneuver me some more.*

A tap sounded on the door.

I walked over to the bookcase and grabbed a book, waving it in front of my face. Time to cool off.

His mother, the Prime Minister, stuck her head through the doorway. At least I recognized her this time, and it was an instant cold shower. I clasped my hands over the book and clutched it to my chest, hoping I wasn't holding a ridiculous title. I put on an innocent expression.

The Prime Minister was wearing a business suit, like always, and a Parliament-negotiating expression. "Wythe, darling. Do get back to my secretary with the name of your date for the end of season ball. I really shouldn't have to remind you again."

"I won't be attending that, Mother." His voice was firm and bored, as if he'd had this conversation with her all year.

The PM's expression hardened, like she was a judge and her will was the gavel. "Oh, but you will. And, you'll need a date."

"Were I to go, and I'm not saying I would, a date would not be a problem," Wythe said.

What did *that* mean? Did he have a girlfriend? If so, wouldn't he say something like that? *If I needed a date, I'd just take "Anne" or "Mary."* Or whatever British girl he was seeing. He didn't have a girlfriend. A pleased zing hit me, and the pleasure was way out of proportion to the moment.

"I have a meeting, Wythe. The council is waiting." His mom closed the door, and then she reopened it. "An appropriate date."

"There's always a catch with you."

The Prime Minister rolled her eyes, now looking more like a mom than a leader of the Western world. She focused on me. "You look like a sensible girl."

Delight flushed my cheeks—an end of the season ball. How Cinderella. *I'm in. I'm the suitable date.* That would net me a point. I'd go to Regent Street for the dress. A blue one to set off his eyes. We'd pose together. I'd put that picture on my mantle.

The Prime Minister nodded toward Wythe. "Do find him an appropriate date to take to the Downing Street Palace Ball." With that edict, the leader of Britain left, snapping the door closed on my misunderstanding.

The flush of pleasure drained from me. How deflating. "What's wrong with me as a date?" I wasn't even embarrassed about asking it. It wasn't like he'd rejected me. His mother had. We hadn't even been on a date and my mother-in-law was rejecting me. Mother-in-law? I had to slow the Freud down.

Wythe looked me over. "Opinionated. American. Intern. Then, of course, there's your disdain for my country." His expression was interested, and his words were a challenge.

"I only disdain the scones." Heat built in my face at that untruth. "And the wool. And the lack of ice cubes."

"There you go. Ice cubes are forbidden at a ball." He rubbed his hand on the outside of his thigh. "Wool, not so much, but unlikely in August. Scones could be present. But, also, not likely."

"You'd be with me on this if you tried one of my mom's scones." I wanted him to feed me another scone.

Wythe heaved a sigh. "Live to dream."

"I wonder how many points I'll get for getting you to the ball with an appropriate date? Two? I'd be managing two people, really." I let the greed show in my voice.

"I won't be pimped out for points."

Oh, but he would. "We'll see." I didn't ask him why he didn't already have a girlfriend. I hated when people asked about my non-existent boyfriend. If I had him, I'd mention him. If I didn't mention him, I was pissed at him and didn't want to talk about him anyway. My status on social media?

Mind your own business. Aka, single and free. Aka, caught him chatting up other girls online. At least I'd caught him before we'd gotten too serious. We'd both been seniors, together for six months, and I hadn't known what was holding me back from getting closer to him. Maybe I'd sensed his disloyal side on some level. I knew he didn't melt me the way Wythe's hands on the back of my zipper had melted me. Maybe it was that simple.

Wythe moved over to the desk to plug his laptop in. "If you went with me to the ball, you'd be kicked out of the program for fraternization."

That would be bad. I nodded and changed the subject because if he knew fully how important that intern photo was, he'd have all the power. It wasn't just the photo. My job prospects improved if I finished this internship. The photo was only part of the reason. Well, it was a lot about the photo. But he didn't need to know that. "Did your professor email back?"

"Yeah. You're in."

Mixed feelings about that went through me. School had pulled me back in. Like my graduation hadn't happened or my diploma had been recalled. I'd had nightmares like that. Now I was living it. Living it with a really hot guy. A hot guy in my nightmares. My dreams. My...

"Where'd you go?"

How to answer that without using the word *bed*? I smiled a toothy smile. "Think the credits will transfer to wherever I end up for grad school?" If I went to grad school. That was my best route without a job.

"It's Oxford." Wythe said the University name in that definitive way British people used when they'd named something of the highest echelon. "It'll transfer."

"Of course. Um, at A&M, I was a senior and an Aggie. What am I called as an Oxford student?"

"You'd be a first year. This is the end of the Trinity term. A special extension project."

"Not much of a ring to that. I'll call us Oxies."

"You will not."

"Oh, but I will."

Chapter 9

Wythe, Caroline, their security team, and I entered the dog show through a private back entrance. Why was Caroline with us? Nanny was back at Downing Street with a migraine, and Georgiana's duties had shifted toward Wythe's brother, Zane. I needed the scoop on that, but her shift had left me with the privilege of taking Caroline to the dog show.

A petite, round lady, the event coordinator according to her name badge, rushed over. Brits weren't really rushers. So, it was either the flush of his hotness getting to her or... I couldn't think of any other reason. That had to be it. Wythe looked wonderful in his dark suit, given his awesome build.

Or maybe it was the intimidation factor of our group being accompanied by guards. That could've been it. Or it was the knowledge that the leader of Western Europe had placed her family in her hands, at her event. That could've been it. Or a trifecta.

The coordinator went straight to Wythe and shook his hand, running down the highlights of the show and ignoring the rest of us.

Yep, she thought he was hot. Because, at first, she'd been all quick steps. Now she was leading us down a hallway at a slow crawl. I looked at two of the guards, trying to catch their eyes to see if they saw what I saw. Wythe needed some body-guarding.

The guards were scanning the area, clearly more interested in room safety than personal dynamics. I stepped to the side, letting Caroline get ahead of me. She scooted forward, catching up to Wythe, getting between him and the coordinator. She walked really close to Wythe's leg. He took her hand, swinging it, and Caroline relaxed. So cute. Such a good little chaperone.

The noise of barking dogs hit us first, and then came the visual: row upon row of shiny cages containing glossy-haired, beribboned show dogs.

Caroline stumbled. Her head swiveled from cage to cage, her eyes wide. For the first time since I'd met her, the little girl was mute.

Not so the dogs or their handlers. Their handlers stood on runners sorting doggie hair products and chatting. Snippets of their conversations floated through the air: "shinier coat," "tendency to whine," "ease of training." Enthusiasm filled the owners' voices, and from the energy in the room, the onlookers had equal passion for the topic. "Unlike no other," one lady declared, measuring the length of a Corgi with her hands.

There was a lot of intensity contained within these four walls, and the animals made me miss Trapper. I'd have to video chat with him tonight. He loved video calls. And for once, I was glad I wouldn't see him in person. Had I smelled like this many other dogs when I got home to him, he'd have gone crazy with the barking.

I snapped off a panoramic shot and fired it over to Felicity. She'd be so jealous. Ridiculous that the thought could bring me such satisfaction, but it did. *Ha.*

We passed through a fire door on our way to the arena, and I nodded to the orange flame symbol and then back to the dog cages. "How do the dogs get out if there's an emergency?"

"Don't worry." The event coordinator motioned to a red fire alarm switch. "If the alarm goes off, the cage doors open." She pointed back to an owner pouring designer Swiss Mountain bottled water into her pug's porcelain bone-shaped dish. He licked his nose in return and then slurped some down.

Did dogs prefer bottled water? We gave Trapper tap water. Always had.

"You needn't worry. These priceless creatures are very safe, very well cared for."

Wythe wasn't saying much. This was my first viewing of his public persona since I'd been introduced to the Prime Family on day one. Come to think of it, even on stage, he'd had the least to say.

I tilted my head. Wythe didn't look uncomfortable. But he wasn't at ease, and he didn't seem to be enjoying the noise or the crowd. Not that anyone else could tell that. He was perfectly polite. Maybe that was it. I knew what he looked like when he was interested and engaged. This wasn't it.

We emerged into a traditional arena area with stadium seating. The event coordinator continued to lead us while going on about the breeding and special handling. I yawned deeply and covered the motion with the back of my hand. When the jetlag was finally over, I'd be so happy.

"Just there. That's the seating reserved for special guests." The coordinator paused and waved toward a row of roped-off seats.

I checked her eyes for mockery or some type of inference about the Prime Family's own *special handling*. Nothing came; she just displayed more Wythe-focused professionalism and British reserve.

I yawned again. The fog of jetlag haunted me every overseas trip without fail. It always lasted the full two weeks for me. Just about the time I'd gotten used to the schedule, my grandparents would be shipping me back home.

Then the cycle would start over again, but not as bad.

Wythe leaned toward me on the steps and put his mouth close to my ear.

The feel of him so close perked me right up.

"No more yawning. The press will say you're bored with the event." He'd been trained for public life, and he was right.

"Then order me some tea." I said it like a challenge. There was no drink stand here.

He nodded and motioned to the coordinator. She came running, and he put in the request for teas and a lemonade for Caroline. I liked guys who got things done, who made the improbable possible.

We took our seats in the roped-off private section: one of the guards, Wythe, Caroline, then me. The other guards were down below by the entrances.

When the drinks came, he passed the lemonade to Caroline, who held it with both hands, and gave a warm paper cup to me. The smell of a floral bergamot came through the little plastic lid. Stronger than the Earl Grays at home but still definitely Earl Gray. Tea at Downing Street was served in china cups. This to-go cup reminded me of home and was strangely comforting.

He gave the guard the next cup and took the last one for himself. His manners were effortless, and crazy attractive for that very reason. He didn't need me to tell him how to act. And he'd served us before himself. I wanted to scoot closer.

Caroline pointed, her arm straight out. It caused the cup to tilt in her little hand, spilling her lemonade over the top. "Look at them."

I scooped the cup from her and put it between us, one hand on it for security, my fingers a little wet and sticky now.

"Just look," Caroline said.

Center stage, the judge let go of the Yorkshire terrier's tail and stepped back from the display platform with a nod. The handler lowered the terrier to the artificial turf so he could run in a circle for us to watch. Caroline popped up so she could see better. She took in the action with big eyes and a grin. "He has hair like you."

Wythe shot me one of those side glances.

Chestnut Yorkie. Yep. "Uh. Thanks."

Claps accompanied the terrier's leashed circling.

"And he goes and goes." Caroline hadn't mastered the restrained British enthusiasm yet. But her commentary was mostly to herself and didn't require input from us.

I turned to Wythe. "The British love their dogs and their gardens."

He wore a polite interested expression while watching the show, and he arched one eyebrow at me. Something lit in his eyes when he looked at me. "Correct."

"At some point, my ancestors left their dogs behind, or

did the Quakers bring them over on a boat?"

"They took them."

"Right. They love them. Then how come my parents never let me have more than one dog growing up?"

His eyes flashed. "Unfathomable."

"Trapper's an exceptional dog. He's a Japanese Chin, and the smartest dog ever." I wasn't really bragging about my dog—who was totally brag-worthy. I was challenging him, engaging him.

"No doubt."

Caroline turned to me, her blue eyes big. "I haven't even one dog."

I showed her a picture of Trapper on my phone, and she made the appropriate appreciative noises. I showed Wythe, too. He arched both eyebrows and nodded. But he didn't share anything from his phone. Either he'd never had a dog and he didn't know this was his key to cue up a cute Internet picture, or the social cues differed from America.

I tipped my teacup at him. "Half full or half empty?" I was really asking how he was handling the event. Was he enjoying it at all? Would it be easy to get him to two more events? Would an offer of two kisses work?

One side of his mouth quirked. "Haven't you heard the old engineering answer to that question?"

I looked him up and down. Rich kid. "It doesn't matter as long as someone else is pouring it?"

He bit his lip and thumped the half-full cup. "The glass isn't half full or half empty. The cup needs a redesign."

When he talked to me, he tilted his body toward mine. I caught his gaze and knew I was smiling at him, not the event. I'd wanted to engage him, but his charm was sucking me in.

I jerked away. *Cameras. Public. Don't get caught staring at the guy.* It was hard not to, because there was a lot I wanted to explore there.

I turned back to the stage. Despite the importance of Wythe's family name, no one had bothered us, but I could tell they knew who Wythe and Caroline were. When we'd come up the steps, the people in the closest seats had stiffened and stared at Wythe and Caroline, glanced away, and then stared again. Those in the seats in front of us did it, too. We kept our gazes on the event.

In the ring, the tiny terrier was replaced with an enormous Irish setter led around in a fast circular trot by a man in a navy suit. The setter's golden hair flew back in bouncing waves with a controlled abandon I could never achieve. The jingle for a popular shampoo ad flashed through my head and stuck. Grr. I needed earbuds and a tune to wash this one away fast. My fingers twitched toward my pocket, but I knew it wasn't appropriate to plug in. Not when half the crowd aimed their cellphone cameras our way. I pulled my public smile back on.

We sat through ten more dogs before Caroline squirmed. Her gaze went to the door we'd come in through. "I want to pet the bunches of dogs."

Wythe lifted her up, and her yellow petticoat puffed over his jacket sleeve. He motioned for me and strode done the steps toward the door.

Caroline was spoiled. But I sort of liked that he gave in to his sister. I only had the one sibling and getting my own way had been a fight from day one. College had brought distance, but not enough.

We went back through to the holding area and once we

got near the puppy cages, Caroline wriggled free. A guard moved into place near her.

I didn't know how puppies fit in with the show, or if they were being sold. I'd have asked the handler, but Wythe motioned for me to join him.

When I got near, he backed away, leading me two rows over. We reached the side wall in a less trafficked area. He looked down at me. "I realized that I should have insisted on my kiss before we left."

His words woke me up better than the tea had. He was thinking about me. And a kiss. Had to love that. A smile wanted to curl on my lips, but I refused to let it. "What? This place doesn't exude romance to you?" I moved closer, partly to be near him and breathe in his yummy cologne, and partly to get out of the way of the tall blonde handler heading up the aisle with two lumbering Great Danes. One Great Dane was always enough.

Wythe's mouth twitched. "Oh, but it does."

I sniffed at the freshly shampooed dog air. "Uh huh. Is that eucalyptus or lemongrass?" A new handler came through escorting blue-eyed Siberian huskies. The myriad of dogs that filled the area was more than I'd ever seen or imagined seeing: beige to red to black; pocket-sized to outweighing me. "You've got to admit it's a cool event."

Wythe brushed his fingers over the top of my shoulder. "Do I?"

It wasn't an overly familiar gesture, just a touch. But it made me want to press his hand there to really feel his fingers press against me. I swallowed. "Well, not number stuff on the computer fascinating. But fascinating."

"Fascinating." Wythe was looking at me, not at the dogs.

And his bright gaze lured me in.

I was looking at him and not the cages full of puppies. He was more captivating than the puppies. I was so in trouble.

What was it about him? He wore a navy jacket with khaki trousers—normal but formal guy clothes, nothing extraordinary. He fit in. The lighter-color trousers marked him as an onlooker. The guards, the staff, and the owners all wore dark trousers with their suits. Britain had uniforms within uniforms. Wythe did look great though. Better than any guy here. He was tall, broad-shouldered, had a narrow waist. I knew he ran with his brother. And he had a gym. What else did he like?

A lady carrying a chow bumped into me from behind. "Excuse me." She wore a frumpy navy suit, and her attention was solely on her dog, who was too big to be carried.

Caroline gave a high-pitched squeal, jumping up and down in front of narrow tan yippy dogs I couldn't identify. Her periwinkle dress swung, showing the yellow petticoats that bounced against the top of her bobby socks.

The handler pointed to a cage full of white fluffy puppies. Caroline clapped and squeaked out praise we could hear from where we stood.

"Your sister thinks this is cool."

"She's six."

"She—"

The guard nearest Caroline tapped on his earpiece. He moved toward her and at the same time held his hands straight up and tapped his fingertips into the palm of his other hand—the signal for an emergency exit.

Emergency.

Danger. My heartbeat picked up.

Dogs.

Kids.

What? Fire?

Energy rushed through me. *Large crowd. Dangerous situation. Bad. Bad. Bad. Fix it. Help.* Where had that exit been in this old building?

"Wythe." Strain sounded in my voice.

Wythe moved to Caroline. The guard was already there, reaching for the little girl. Caroline leaned over the side of the cage and snagged a fluffy white puppy. She was balanced by her belly on the top edge of the cage, her feet kicking. "I got one. I'll save it."

Her guard scooped her and the cotton ball puppy into his arms and headed for the exit.

Wythe shifted direction and ran back to me.

Wythe was running. Not out with his brother. Not on a treadmill in the family gym. In public. In panic? *Bad. Bad. Bad. Fight the adrenaline. Think.* I threw myself toward the wall, scratching along the painted concrete block walls, feeling for the red fire switch. I jerked the lever down.

Chapter 10

Alarms blared. A blue light flashed. Howls and barking pierced the air. The latches on the cages around me released. Three sheepdogs bolted for freedom, their hair bouncing like mops. Three ran straight out, and two circled me and Wythe, herding us toward the corner.

I pushed at the sturdy, black and sable-colored dog. "Move."

Wythe broke past the largest. "Come on." He lifted me up and over the dog and tossed me over his shoulder, firefighter style. My midsection rammed into him and my breath left my body. Wow. Crazy. This so could have been a moment. His hand. My butt. But I couldn't even go there. All I could concentrate on was the madhouse around me and the need to suck air into my lungs.

I wiggled to get a breath.

I braced myself against the long muscles of his back, looking at the scurrying guests and the frantic pet owners chasing their pampered and shampooed show dogs. Bejeweled leashes hung from their hands as they called for "Mr. Potkins" and "Royal Alfa Four."

The dogs themselves shook off their training, resorted to their feral instincts, and bolted free to race around the room. Each displayed traits of their breeds: herding dogs herded, yappy dogs yapped, and they all ran.

Wythe skirted around a lady, trying to coax a Chihuahua from under a bleacher with a treat. This wasn't a time for coaxing. "Grab him and run," I screamed at her. "He's going to fry."

That earned me a startled look and a frown. I felt chastised and self-righteous at the same time. I was trying to save her.

Wythe sped up. We bolted from the back entrance and tumbled into the limo. Caroline and her guard were already inside.

Wythe checked her seatbelt.

Before the outside guard got the door shut behind us, the car rolled into motion, pulling away from the building, jolting me against the seat.

What the heck had just happened? I pulled on my own seatbelt and drew in a deep breath, rubbing my abdomen, which had taken a pounding during the amateur firefighter carry. I looked back through the window. Show people and dogs streamed from the exit. "Are they going to be okay? Should we direct them or something? Fit them in here with us?"

Caroline's guard tapped his earpiece. "It wasn't a fire, Miss. Just a family drill. The dogs will be fine."

Wythe huffed out an audible breath and looked away, his shoulders tense, his body still. Then he looked me over, as if making sure I was okay.

I gave him a reassuring smile. He seemed about to say

something, but Caroline made a noise, drawing our attention to her.

Caroline hugged the saved white puppy to her chest. "I got one. I got one. I saved it," Caroline said, her cheeks flushed and her eyes a vivid triumphant blue. The white fluffy puppy had triangular ears. The only color on him came from his shiny black eyes and nose. If the poached dog had a mouth, I couldn't see it.

"That's a teacup Pomeranian, miss," the guard said, double-checking the door locks.

"I will call him Teacup."

"Yes, Miss."

"See, Wythe?" Caroline held the puppy up and wiggled him.

The upset emotions faded from his eyes, and his face softened as he looked at his little sister.

I liked that about him. I didn't know what I felt about the security drill. I guess a sick relief that it was a false alarm. We weren't hurt. The dogs weren't hurt. I needed to focus on the positive. Wythe and I had almost shared a moment. Plus, I'd gotten him there painlessly, which meant my first intern point had landed in my lap.

I had to check my status. That uptick would help me chill. Surely, my point would have posted by now. Could I snip a screenshot of my success and email it to my sister? That would really improve my mood. I logged into my status on the intern.co.uk.gov portal that had been set up for our use.

Wythe looked over my shoulder. "Really? We narrowly escaped with our lives and you're checking on your status?" His voice sounded dry, not amused, not irritated. Just dry.

"It's important. I did my job. Got you to the dog show. I'll get a point." I wasn't hiding it from him. He needed to know this internship mattered to me and I appreciated his help. He'd gone to the event for me, and that helped my status. I clicked on my steaming egg. Zero points still hovered over the fat end of the egg. I frowned.

Why? Why did the pointed end balance on the ground and the fat end wave about in the air? That wasn't how eggs worked. That wasn't how gravity worked. *Zero. Zed. Zip.* "Guess they haven't updated the charts yet."

An area alert notification popped up on my phone. British news alert. Pictures of running dogs flooded the screen. But there, in the corner... I tapped on the photo. A picture of my butt blew up in the image.

Wythe read over my shoulder, "Prime Minister's son saves onlooker as dog show turns into a melee."

I double clicked a second post from the show. This one also featured Wythe's hand on my butt. This one was captioned, *Bummer at the Royal Dog Show.* Awesome. Online news was quick.

Wythe's mouth twisted. "You're smiling. You're not put out?"

"Please. Your big old hand makes my butt look small. I'm framing it." I could remember how his hand on me had felt every time I looked at the picture. Not that I had really been able to enjoy it in the running, panicked exit. But I could roll the image around in my mind later. I smiled to myself and clicked again, but the rest of the shots were of dogs and their handlers. Some action running shots that were pretty funny, and some were suit-wearing owners clutching their canines as they gave soundbites.

I showed Caroline a shot of the puppies. She looked, but all her focus was really on Teacup, petting him, reassuring him. Adorable.

We were almost back at Downing Street when an email notification flashed on my screen. I read aloud, "Email from Peppa: Due to the press incident, anticipate an immediate transfer upon return." My voice thinned, and my insides sank.

Peppa had done it. She'd gotten me shifted off this assignment. Just like she'd wanted from day one. It physically hurt. The pain was either in reaction to the cessation of the adrenaline, being carried over Wythe's shoulder, or sheer annoyance at the email... I didn't know the exact reason, but it felt bad. Peppa had tried to boot me before. It hadn't worked then. Now, she was seizing an opportunity. Like I had. This was just business for her.

Wythe rubbed his hand over his mouth, still leaning against my shoulder. He had been reading. Now he was...what...comforting me? Sharing space with me? Commiserating? What did his closeness mean?

Snap out of it. He was European. It meant they stood and sat and talked all while too close. It was what they did. It meant nothing. It was their norm. I was thinking way too much about him. I checked the traffic. Seemed normal for London. Full, and no one driving on the sidewalk to escape the Capital. "It really was just a drill."

The guard glanced from Caroline and her squirming Pomeranian to me and a frowning Wythe. "The dog show wasn't the tamest event to attempt a drill."

Drill was good. Drill meant safety. I'd pulled a public fire alarm on a drill. Was that even legal? Was ignorance of the drill an excuse? My stomach sank. That did sound like a transfer-worthy offense.

***

I didn't get the word until that evening. Peppa opened the door to the Prime Family's sitting room where I sat with Wythe and Caroline. "The prime secretary is handling the backlash from the incident. You needn't be transferred if there is an adequate apology from you to the Kennel Club. You will apologize to the Kennel Club. Personally. That would be most appropriate. An in-person apology."

Okay. No thanks. I'd write a letter.

Peppa was eying me down like I was her trash can, and she could dump her garbage on me. Wythe hadn't bothered looking at Peppa. Caroline was engrossed in petting a sleeping Teacup. Peppa was focused on me. It was just me and Peppa in a stare-off. If she thought she'd put me in a car and drive me back to the dog show, she could think again. Avoidance was key. I'd never be available when the car pulled around. *Pressing duties. So sorry.* Then the dog show would be over, and I'd be off the hook.

Peppa opened the door wide.

She could throw down a red carpet. I wasn't following her lead.

Peppa grinned by rolling her lips inward. "Come in."

A man in a pressed brown suit holding a gold and white long-haired dog entered. The dog's bangs were tied up high in a ponytail. I brushed my own hair away from my hot face.

The round petite woman behind him carried a similar-sized dog that had a scrunched face and golden fur. She wore a dark suit with a red scarf. They all smelled like the fancy strawberry dog shampoo.

The dogs' heads swiveled, eying Teacup as if they were expecting a fight but were too well bred to kick up a fuss.

Teacup, for his part, slept through their entrance. But Caroline kept him close.

"Welcome to Downing Street," Peppa said.

Names were exchanged, along with Kennel Club titles. Drinks were offered and refused. The Kennel Club guy took the lead and started in the second the pleasantries were done, "We hope you understand we hold Downing Street responsible for this unfortunate incident." His accent sounded posher than any audio I'd heard of the royal family.

"Very unfortunate," Peppa said, sounding just like him.

I barely resisted rounding out my cheeks to round out my words. Barely. But I resisted. If the point system knew how much I restrained myself, I'd be on the top tier. Floating above top tier. Like a superior intern angel. "I'm truly sorry. I was trying to ensure everyone evacuated safely." I'd been practicing those words since I got Peppa's text about transferring me.

"It's really unforgivable," Peppa said.

"Is it, Peppa?" Wythe's tone was hard.

Peppa looked away.

The female handler shifted her scrunch-faced dog and held it away from her body, so we'd get a good look. "They're ruined!" she said in a French accent. She plopped the dog on the rug, square on a daffodil, and hooked her diamond-encrusted leash over her narrow wrist. Her motions had a snappy quality, in case we weren't getting her frustration from her words.

We were getting it.

The man frowned at her foreign emotionalism, shook his head, and turned back to us. He pursed his lips Britishly. "There were some unfortunate couplings as a result of the cage doors being released."

Oh. That was unforgivable. No touching.

Wythe glanced between the two primped dogs. "Hideous," he muttered in an aside to me.

The man stared hard at Wythe. "I assume Downing Street will assume responsibility should there be any unfortunate issue?"

Wythe nodded in that British man-of-his-word way.

The man nodded back. The matter settled, the two turned to leave.

Peppa rushed to get the door.

The woman spoke in a spattering of French that involved using her hands, which jerked the leash she held, and ended her words in English. "Some breeds should not mix."

Wythe stared hard at the two dogs, as if trying to discern a difference. "Aren't they the same thing?"

The woman turned at his question and snapped, "This is a Pekingese. That is a Shi Zhu."

The male handler looked appalled.

Wythe moved closer. "God awful."

The woman followed the man, muttering about "shedding" and "barking."

I couldn't hear what he said, but his tone sounded defensive. As they left, Caroline returned and Peppa walked the handlers out.

My gaze remained glued to the departing fluffy dogs. "I want one."

"Me, too," Caroline said, petting her own fluffy white dog with small untiring pats that the dog curved into. "A friend for Teacup."

Caroline was sitting on the floor with her back to the desk leg. I sat beside her and petted the puppy, who'd fallen asleep again. He was soft, silky, so sweet. "Was that a good enough apology, or will Peppa still try and get me transferred?"

"Transfers happen," Caroline said.

"Not this time, it won't," Wythe said.

Pleasure at his reassurance flitted through me. We were a good duo. Solid.

Wythe shrugged one shoulder. "I still need you on my final project."

Ah. Literature class. How deflating. Which was ridiculous. I should not feel deflated. He did not have that power over me. The power to wound with an absent word. No.

Peppa returned.

"This is my private study, is it not?" Wythe sounded as put out as the dog owners.

"Sorry, Wythe," Peppa said. "I thought it would be less traumatic for Miss Caroline if I was the one to return the puppy."

What?

Chapter 11

Peppa wanted to take Caroline's puppy. Caroline understood Peppa's words instantly in the way only a little child could. She screamed and clutched the dog to her chest.

Teacup yowled.

Wythe's face stilled.

"Your mother thinks it's best that I return him straightaway." Peppa took the dog from Caroline and walked out.

I ran after her, all out, like she had the key to the top of the photo stand and all I had to do was reach her to win it. *Get your hands off that dog.* "Wait up," I huffed.

"The handlers are downstairs. They've agreed to return him to his proper owners. Frankly, that will be a relief. Keep our hands out of it. Good for all concerned."

"I'll take him." I wanted to screech at her, but I stuck my hands out and took him as if she agreed with me. "I want to give that apology another go, like you said, so I can keep my post." I sounded totally fake to my own ears.

Peppa seemed to accept the groveling without hesitation.

"Of course." She wiped white fur from her lapel, looking toward Wythe's study where we could still hear Caroline crying. She went the other way.

I petted Teacup. "Sorry about that."

Teacup licked my hand with a tiny swipe, curled on his side, and kicked his little padded feet against my palm. My heart melted like one of Katniss's flame dresses. Poof. Teacup liked it here. The only thing preventing him from staying were rules and regulations. Rules and regulations around a puppy. So silly.

Caroline spun around the corner, screeching. She halted when she saw I had the puppy and stopped right in front of me. She didn't grab for him though. She hugged me around the waist. I bent and scooped her up. She was heavier than she looked. Caroline hooked one arm around my neck and took the puppy with the other.

Teacup, for his part, didn't seem to mind the drama. He just wanted his cuddle.

"So, I figure, we talk to Nanny."

Caroline hiccupped and sniffed. "Yeah. Talk to Nanny."

"We tell her how we'll lay down puppy pads, so Teacup won't damage the carpets."

"Yeah."

"And we'll put kibble in his bowl."

"Yeah." She sniffed again. "Every day. And he can have a water bowl, too. Shaped like a bone." She lay her head on my shoulder.

This was the kind of sister I could love. I mean, I loved my sister. But it should've been like this. Teaming up together against the outside world. Not making it worse for each other.

I got to the family hall and hesitated, my arms dragging at the kid's weight. I had no clue where her nanny disappeared to when she wasn't around. She was just a dapper middle-aged lady in a gray uniform with a white apron who appeared when Caroline needed to be taken away from adult talk. Maybe there was a speed dial number for her, or an emergency call button on the wall.

Caroline pointed as if she understood that I didn't know where to go. I followed her directions. Her play room was similar in size to her brother's study, but it held enough pastel-colored kids' stuff that it seemed like hers.

Nanny wasn't there. But Georgiana sat on an overstuffed yellow armchair with a teapot in front of her and a tray of small cakes. She was feeding a pastel pink, gold-dusted macaroon to a really hot guy. He bore enough of a resemblance to Wythe that I knew this had to be their older brother, Zane.

Zane nodded at Georgiana. "Another."

Georgiana giggled and shook her head, her cheeks flushed, her attention totally on him.

My eyebrows arched. Caroline called out, "Zane, Ms. Georgiana, Look what I got. Miss Kira got him for me."

Georgiana's gaze lit on the puppy. "Oh. Cute."

I put Caroline down.

Zane got up and strode toward us. His blue eyes narrowed at me, but he said nothing. He ruffled the puppy's head, and then Caroline's. "Good for you, Poppet." He stared hard at me. "That won't cause a fight at all." He had a deep overeducated voice, like Wythe. He strode from the room with Georgiana watching him and Caroline cooing over the puppy.

I wanted to warn Georgiana. Zane looked like trouble, but I'd seen her expression enough on my friends' faces over the years that I knew the warning was too late. "I thought you were off Caroline duty."

"Mostly I'm wrangling Zane." Georgiana's lips quirked up. "But Nanny persists in calling me in. And I'm not great at saying no."

I got it. A team probably was best when watching Caroline.

Caroline went to the striped sofa and curled up. "Yes. Miss Georgiana. His name is Teacup and Kira got him for me."

Well. Sort of.

Georgiana grinned at me. "Well."

"Yep," I said.

Caroline nodded slowly while petting the white fluff ball. "Oh, yes. We have to hide him from the bad people."

I winced.

Caroline sniffled and held the puppy up to her face. "Take my picture. Like you did with Trapper and send it to me. Please."

I hadn't heard her use that word before. I took her picture as she smiled big. I sat beside her, showing her the photo.

A tap sounded on the door.

Wythe stood on the threshold, rapping on the doorframe with the knuckles of one hand and holding the black porcelain Egyptian figurine in the other.

Caroline's eyes grew wider.

"I see you don't need this," Wythe said.

"I do," Caroline said, her voice hushed and intense.

Wythe took the figurine over to the mantle and placed it up there. I had the impression that if Caroline weren't holding a real dog right now, the priceless, fragile artifact would be in her little hands. Wythe joined us, brushed a finger over the puppy, and then tapped the tip of Caroline's nose, making her giggle.

They were so cute.

I leaned in with them and snapped the photo, while hoping the selfie didn't show how gooey he was making me.

"You saved the dog, I see," Wythe said. His tone was somewhat mocking, but his gaze said he appreciated me. In a different way than he'd appreciated me before.

Heat hit my cheeks, but I felt strongly about this, too. "If they won't let her have Teacup, I can keep him for her. He's not big. I'll hide him in my sock drawer."

Caroline giggled. "No. In mine. Ms. Georgiana will hide him, too."

"All that hair on my clothes?" Georgiana held up her hands, palms forward. "No thank you. I'll leave the hiding to you two."

Caroline popped up and ran over to her. "But he is so cute."

Georgiana pulled her up, and Caroline curled into her side. "He is. I'm sure he won't be a bother."

"Oh, he won't be," Caroline said. "Teacup is so good."

"I can see that," Georgiana said.

Wythe rose, in one of those smooth enviable motions. "I'm going for a run. If there's any more trouble, call me. Caro's keeping that dog." His tone was certain and strong.

Feeling chemistry with him was one thing. A crush was one thing...but he was more than a crush-worthy good-looking guy. He was sweet, strong, and loyal. My heart stopped and then pounded. I did not want this. Dizziness hit me, and I clasped my arms over my knees.

He left the room, not knowing what he'd left behind.

One melting heart.

Chapter 12

Felicity buzzed me. *I am so close to that top spot. I'll probably make head intern. How are you doing with all the rain? Been up to Nottingham yet?*

Too busy.

Ha. As what? Paper Runner? Felicity ended that with a snickering emoji.

Did she think she was being funny? She was such a...

A picture of her sitting in the Rose Garden popped up.

She was so annoying. I could so freaking top a picture of her with a sterling purple rosebush. I shot her the picture of me, Caro, Wythe, and Teacup. *#New Puppy.*

Top that, Trapper Keeper. I hit silence on the phone so I wouldn't be sucked into more back and forth and tapped on the door before going into Wythe's room.

Wythe sat in his window seat, typing away at his laptop. He wore pressed navy trousers and a white buttoned-down shirt, though it was Sunday.

I held onto my resolve. I was not falling for him. I'd dressed extra casually to prove it to myself. I was wearing navy, too. Navy sweats and a white concert t-shirt. "What are you doing?" That was a normal question. I'd ask anyone that. I wasn't dying for the answer.

"Participating in social media." Wythe hit the keyboard with loud taps and read aloud as he typed, "Dining on sticky toffee pudding. Tasty. Cook's spot on today."

I liked how he said the word "tasty." I checked the empty side tables and the desk. No sign of a plate. "You're not eating pudding. Or anything, for that matter."

"No. But I *want* sticky toffee pudding. And now everyone will harass Cook for the recipe. I anticipate many desserts coming our way as Cook refines his pudding to share it with the world."

"How manipulative. And delicious." I stepped closer to check his screen. "Really? That's a lot of followers."

"PR set it up. They don't love it that I use it to my advantage. But really. What did they expect?"

Forty people followed me. I made a sighing, envious sound, but I didn't really care. Loads of followers weren't my goal. I should have a goal. Maybe decide between a job and graduate school. Figure it out so I wouldn't be stuck at my parents' house in the fall. For now, I was taking a break from thinking about it. Felicity didn't have to think about it. She had a plan. She'd majored in business and stayed in America.

My mood took a dive.

Wythe glanced up at me and arched one eyebrow.

He noticed my mood. He cared. My heart panged. No. I was not that into him. I was just homesick, not heartsick. I touched the screen. "Can you type something about your cook going through a TexMex phase?"

He shuddered.

I leaned into his shoulder and put my lips to his ear, breathing in his yummy cologne. "Please."

He swallowed, and his fingers moved against the keyboard. *You didn't hear it from me, but I heard that Cook is desperately looking for authentic Tex-Mex recipes. Might you send him some?*

That was fun. I kissed his cheek with a grin on my lips, as if my heart weren't pounding. I was just being playful. "You just gained a new follower."

Wythe glanced up with a glint in his eyes.

It stilled me. It lured me. "Um. I've got to go…" I couldn't think of more of an excuse than that. I needed to leave, but I couldn't move.

Wythe put his computer down and rose to his feet.

Looking at Wythe standing there made my insides tingle. I wanted him here, up against me. How would he feel? How would he touch me? How would he taste? Did he kiss wildly like his eyes or contained like his demeanor?

As if he heard my thoughts, he moved toward me.

I backed toward the wall.

This couldn't be good. I had to talk myself down. He was way too handsome. That was it. I drew in a breath. *Brace. Brace.* Spoiled hot guys could rarely kiss. They didn't know how to put in the effort. They liked to lie back and be adored.

Wythe's mouth softened. And he looked straight into my eyes. All focus on me.

Those eyes. Last winter, I'd stared for hours at the blue chem logs burning in our fireplace. The blue-green flame had fascinated me. Wythe fascinated me the same way. I pushed off the wall and took a step closer to him.

His hands touched my face—warm, calloused, more in line with his eyes than his manner. He pressed his whole body against me, creating a flow of liquid anticipation.

This was happening.

I grabbed his shoulders. He was hard, solid, and firm in my dissolving world. Dissolving thoughts, dissolving knees, him...

I curled my fingers in, holding onto him, urging him...

He kissed me. His lips were certain and soft, then rough, and then soft. He touched his tongue to mine. Ah. He tasted like... I don't know. Something forbidden, delicious, and so sexy. He pulled back and looked at me. I looked at him. *More.*

Liquid heat melted me, flowed under my skin, spreading sensation from my lips to my toes. I wanted to analyze it. I wanted to stay here longer and feel.

He ran his fingertips from my shoulders to my palms. Where he touched me, traced me, electric zings were spurred by the melting happening inside me. "Kira." His voice was deep, and his eyes had darkened.

I went from holding on to suddenly restless. I needed to feel him. Not the cotton of his shirt but him.

I ran my hands down his back to his waist. The shirt frustrated me and blocked me from touching his skin.

He repeated the gesture on me. His hands were firm on my waist, and he dipped his thumbs under the hem of my shirt, touching my waist. It was a shock, a small pleasurable shock that circled through to my core. I loved it.

I slipped my hands up over his chest and around his neck, clinging to him. He gripped my hips and then palmed my backside, lifting me. I wrapped my thighs around his waist, locking my ankles. He walked me back and then I was down.

My palms hit the floral window seat cushion, and I maneuvered myself back. He leaned into me. Following me.

I broke away for a gasp of air, and his mouth moved to my neck. I breathed in as the sensation created new sparks inside me that wanted his lips to melt them, too. Holy crap.

I lay back and pushed back on the cushion. He followed me down.

His weight. His presence... Him... This was like nothing I'd ever felt and was everything I'd ever wanted to feel.

A knock sounded on the door.

Chapter 13

Wythe raised his head.

I pressed my lips together, missing the press of his lips.

His gaze was longing. And he was looking at me. He touched my cheek.

Ah. I breathed out and reached up. I slid my hands over his biceps, squeezing.

The taps grew louder.

The door. The knocking. People. I muffled a sound and slapped his arm when all I wanted was to grab on. "Go." My voice came out husky, and the word lacked force. *Stay.*

He paused and rubbed his thumb over my bottom lip, making me shiver.

"I'll have to think of a new bribe," I said, trying to lighten the mood but failing because my voice came out breathless and it didn't match my emotions.

His eyes darkened, and he put his lips to my ears. "You don't need a bribe." His voice was deep and sexy. "If you want a kiss, take it." He strode to the fireplace, leaving me, but was still looking at me. Wythe. Son of the UK Prime Minister. Head of State.

No touching.

I smoothed my shirt down and shifted into an innocent picture pose. Knees together, feet swinging over the side. It felt wrong to be apart.

Wythe turned and stared into the fireplace. Would getting caught kissing me result in repercussions for him? Probably. I know it would for me.

Another knock sounded on the door, this time more forceful. And this time, the door opened.

In came Peppa in one of her gray suits with a woman I hadn't met. Tall, brunette, dark yellow dress. Thirties. She was smiling as much as Peppa was frowning. No, not smiling, the woman was beaming.

At me.

Go away. I did not want to deal with Peppa and a stranger. I wanted to deal with Wythe. To think about that kiss. Could it even be called a kiss? It was unlike any kiss I'd ever had. Better. More spark. More interest in taking it further. More. This was something to explore.

The beaming woman was making a path right to me, not allowing me my thoughts. "Is this her?"

This couldn't be right...or good. I hadn't done anything beam-worthy. The lady turned to Wythe, shining a smile on him, but it wasn't a lit-up smile; it was oil-slick shiny. Something lurked beneath it, and I wanted no part of it. Like those documentaries of the ocean. Who wanted to know about all those creatures down there? Not me. I wanted to swim in the ocean in ignorant bliss.

The lady said, "Brilliant."

Not brilliant.

Wythe went from smiling to frowning to still-faced. He greeted the lady with a nod. "Marsha."

"Just oh-so-brilliant, you." Marsha wagged her finger at me. "But all press, every little bit, goes through me. Sorry." She walked forward and offered her hand. "Marsha Ovem. U.K. Public Relations."

P.R. My mind raced through all the social media possibilities. Was this about the dog show? Wythe's online recipe hunting? I seized that answer because it had little to do with me. My shoulders relaxed. I was getting praised for the summer dessert debate. "Sticky Toffee Pudding getting a lot of hits?"

"All Wythe's recipe requests receive a surprisingly large number of hits." Marsha's expression was calculating, like the glint in her brown eyes. She wasn't truly in the throes of happiness. She was thinking, processing, manipulating.

That's what it was. Her expression reminded me of Felicity whenever one of my sister's schemes worked. Like when she'd gotten Mom to buy her a more expensive prom dress than her half of the budget allowed. Mom's favorite saying was sometimes Felicity got the bigger slice of pie, sometimes I did. But it wasn't true. Felicity mostly did.

Something was going on here, too. This meeting had an underlying suspense to it that made me cringe.

Marsha grinned at Peppa, her whitened teeth still at a 100-watt voltage. I wished she'd turn it down a notch. She was ruining the concept of a smile. Marsha held up three fingers. "Peppa, head intern here, tells me that all you new interns need at least three points by summer's end to be a part of the intern photo."

Peppa held up three fingers also, and then slowly rolled down her ring and middle finger, leaving her index finger raised. "Kira has one point." Peppa hadn't been able to take it away, despite the dog show drama.

"Yeah." I sounded wary. I raised my own index finger. It seemed like the thing to do in this situation.

Marsha rubbed her hands together. "And they are really extraordinarily difficult to attain."

Impossible without Wythe's compliance, but they would have been easy to get if he were the kind of guy who loved the spotlight. He wasn't. "Yeah."

"Well, I get to be the one who shares the very good news. You, my dear, have earned your next point. And it's a big, fat hopping one." She held up two fingers in a 'V' for a victory gesture. She poked them toward the sky. "That's two big ones for you."

My insides flipped. "Uh. I don't see how…"

"A pet." Marsha shook her head. "Really. I've been pushing the idea of a Scottish-fold kitten on the PM for ages. But I got shot down. Every. Time." Marsha patted the side of her head with her palm, as if her shaking it had jostled her braids. It hadn't. "But you…" She pointed her finger at me, so everyone knew she was talking about me. "Going to Miss Caroline directly…" She clapped, her gestures growing big with her words. "With a puppy! Brilliant." She wagged her finger again. "But I'm not just here to award your point. I need you to acknowledge that you've had a little gentle reminder. All press, every bit of it, goes through me."

I wasn't getting something here, and it left me confused and leery. Not a good feeling. I tilted my head. "I acknowledge all press goes through you." *Please, go away now.*

"*Kitman Carrying On*. Clever. Two Ks together would have been better. Like *Kitman Kicking It* or some such. But as a tagline, it's good. Catchy."

Kitman Carrying On was Felicity's screen title for her blog. It all coalesced in my brain as I got it. My insides went cold with knowledge and dread. This was about Felicity. She put her personal stuff on the Internet all the time, pictures of her meals, her thoughts and selfies. And on a few regrettable occasions, when she wanted to face me yelling at her, she put my business out there. Now I was really worried.

Marsha handed her phone to Wythe, and he scrolled to the next screen.

I rolled my lips together. "May I see it?" I shook my head. "Never mind." I grabbed my phone. I seldom checked Felicity's feed, but I knew how to get to there. I scrolled for her newest posts.

There it was. Felicity had cropped the picture I'd sent her. It only showed little Caroline and the puppy. And she'd posted it for thousands of likes and resends. How could she do that?

My breath halted. I popped my head up. Marsha was looking at me. Peppa was looking at me. Wythe was looking at me.

Marsha nodded enthusiastically. "We'll be doing weekly features with the puppy. You know as he…" She waved her hand. "Explores the garden, sniffing British flowers and such. Without Miss Caroline, of course. We don't use her for photo ops."

Wythe's expression was flat. I looked back down at my phone.

I hit the next picture and my insides went from flipping

to hurting. Me and Wythe. This time, Felicity had cropped Caroline and the puppy out. *Why, Felicity? Why do this to me?*

Wythe was gorgeous in the photo. I loved his expression. I loved the picture of us together, but it was misleading.

My gaze flew to him. His eyes burned hard, straight at me. But not in a good way. Not like before. I'd never seen them like this. He turned and left the room. Leaving me with Peppa and Marsha, even though this was his study.

Oh, no.

My insides cringed. He was the only one I wanted to explain myself to right now. I ran past them and chased him down the hall. "Wait."

He stopped and looked straight through me.

"Wythe."

His chest was rising and falling, faster than normal. He turned and kept walking. Straight to Caroline's room. Every cell in my body urged me to follow him.

The PM was in there talking to Caroline. She looked from me to Caroline. "So, whose puppy is this?"

Caroline clutched the dog to her chest and scooted to the edge of the sofa. "Mine."

Her little determined expression broke my heart. "It can be mine if he needs to be," I said.

Wythe didn't look at me. He moved beside his sister. "That's Caro's puppy, and she's keeping him." His words were firm and flat.

The PM seemed startled but nodded. She glanced at me in the doorway and gave me a nod that I returned.

Wythe didn't. It was like I wasn't there to him. It hurt. It was new, and it hurt. He needed a second to cool off. And

109

I needed time to form my explanation. And I needed to step out of this family's business.

I left the room.

***

The new dynamic between me and Wythe lasted days. I spent the first day deleting Felicity's messages. It was easy on day one. I was too angry with her to do anything but delete them. If I responded, I would have said something very mean, the way I did when I lost my temper, and then I'd have felt bad, as if I'd done something wrong, when it was she who'd overstepped.

On day two, I had to move my text notification app to another screen, so it wasn't right there shouting unopened messages at me, forcing me to fight the need to click on them. Why did that little number over the box have that power?

On day three, it was weirdly easy to ignore Felicity's messages altogether. That was the day I started to read the intern orientation packet. I needed to understand Downing Street. Every detailed inch of it. And the recommended U.K.gov websites.

On day four, I got an email from the literature professor. Just a splash of red on a white background. It was the next clue for our literature class. Which we hadn't been working on at all. Class assignments here were weird, structureless. We probably weren't the only ones who hadn't sent in any more literature thoughts, given that the professor was poking us. The timing was perfect because it gave me an excuse to go see Wythe.

Luckily, I still worked here. If Wythe had intended to

kick me out, I'd have known it by now. He hadn't, so I had an ID badge that still got me into his rooms. He was going to deal with me.

Today.

Now.

Determination fueled my strides, and I got down the stairs to the family rooms in record time. Funny how that worked. If I'd been going to do a normal day's work, it would have taken me fifteen minutes longer. Because I was going to see Wythe, who made my heart pound, I got there quickly. I found Wythe in the gym doing pull-ups. He wore black sweats and a short-sleeved shirt. Those arms. So large, muscular, and impressive. He'd lifted me over to the window seat as if I weighed nothing.

He kept going. Up. Down. Up. Down.

I was annoyed with him, but something about watching him work out while I was angry with him was hot.

Up. Down. Up. Down.

I got right in front of him. "You're going to talk to me."

Up. Down. Up. Down.

I pointed at him. "I will make you."

Wythe gave me a look that said I couldn't make him do anything. But then he narrowed his eyes, released the bar, and dropped down to his feet. He grabbed a towel and rubbed it over his face and sweat-damp hair, and then looked at me with his feral blue eyes. "This internship thing. Did they assign you to manipulate me? Or did you do it on your own?" His accent was the same: posh and rounded but rougher somehow.

The questions rocked me to the edge of anger. Fast. With no pause for more complex emotions. Just simple burning anger that had been fuming inside me for days. "Yeah. All internships are like this. We kiss guys to make them obedient. And then post their photos for the thrill of a few thousand likes."

He turned his back on me and moved over to the granite bar that held towels and a water cooler. He grabbed an ice blue sports drink and chugged it.

"It wasn't about you. I was bragging on the puppy because my sister has our dog Trapper with her in D.C." That made it sound almost worse somehow.

He chugged harder, not appeased, but he was looking at me.

I wasn't mad at him. This was misplaced anger. I shut up and closed my eyes.

His suspicions were understandable. I needed to do better.

I went over to him, bracing my hands on top of the cool water tank, and softened my voice. "The *Kitman Carrying On* thing—that's my sister's feed. You can have security check that, confirm it. I didn't post that picture. I wouldn't do that. My sister Felicity did." There. Misunderstanding cleared up.

Or at least it should've been, but I could see from his expression it wasn't. When people were legit wronged, a simple explanation was rarely enough. They'd ride on the wronged-pony-express until enough sorries made them rein in their sulking.

He pointed the almost-empty sports drink at me. "Sure, Kira. But you know, I've been through this before. Guess what happened with Vihaan, my first Oxford partner?"

Oh, no. My hands grew sweaty atop the tank, and I dropped

them to my sides, wiping them on my hips. Was this where the defiant hands-on-hip pose had come from? Someone had put their sweaty hands on their hips because of nerves and then their only choice was to crumple or brace there. I braced there like Wonder Woman assessing an impossible situation.

"It was early. Partners were just starting to post pictures and quotes, so the professor would throw out clues in response. We wanted him to define what he wanted for 'Literature the ultimate.' A paper on the word 'ultimate?' A favorite author? Whatever. Vihaan sold pics of me to the press." Wythe tossed his empty drink bottle in the bin, and I knew my time to convince him was winding down.

"I didn't sell anything." I tried to catch his gaze, but he wasn't looking directly at me. I hated that.

"But you got awarded anyway. With a point. Didn't you?" Wythe shook his head. "I'm done with this." He sounded formal, final, and cold.

That made me feel sick, anxious, and frozen out.

He went over to the intercom phone—the one that called staff.

"Wythe."

"Enjoy your new point. It's the last one you'll get out of me." He sounded like he'd be switching my assignment immediately or tossing me to the street. Guys were better at that—cutting you off totally. And if I were gone, I couldn't reach him again. Not with all his layers of security. This was it. This was my chance.

My head spun, twisting the need to blame my sister into this argument, and I couldn't think. And this stuff with my sister was only part of it. There was the him and me that we also needed to talk about. "Wythe."

He punched numbers into the base of the landline. "I think it will be better if you switch back to, what was it? Paper Runner? That would be best." He was saying it to my face.

I didn't care to hear it. "Wythe."

Was that pleading in my voice? I hated that. I hated how this made me feel. And how dare he pull this on me? This walk-away BS. Anger steamed at my temples... building, building, hazing out reason. Like when Felicity had taken the last of the hand towels at the airport when we left. And the dispenser gave me two inches of thin paper towel and then it wouldn't dispense anymore. I'd cussed it and crawled up on the wet counter to bang on the dispenser. It still hadn't given me more towels. So, then my hands were wet, and the knees of my yoga pants were wet. And I'd just looked stupid. That was me now, angry at this whole thing. And about to do something stupid.

Think.

Think.

I needed more time with him to explain. How?

The mantle candles caught my eye. Their dried wax drippings had cooled along their sides. Real candles. Fire. I reached up and grabbed the tallest, dark-orange candle, sparkle cinnamon. I grabbed the electric lighter. I searched the ceiling for the smoke alarm. It was close enough to the weight bench.

I jogged over and climbed up.

Wythe put down the handset, ending the call he'd been about to make. "What are you doing?"

I ignored his question and lit the candle.

"Kira?"

I held it high, blowing at the small flame, forcing the wisps of heat and dark smoke upward. Warm wax dripped along the back of my fingers and cinnamon fragrance curled through the air.

Wythe stopped asking what I was doing. For an Oxie, he'd taken a while to figure it out. He bit out a curse and strode toward me.

The alarm stayed silent.

I blew harder. *Go off, darn you.* Was I going to have to light a towel on fire? The trash can? I'd do it.

Beep. Beep. Beep. The alarm sounded.

Chapter 14

Wythe put his strong arm around my waist, pulling me off the weight bench to the floor. "Are you mad?"

A little. I was standing close to him, the lit cinnamon candle clutched to my chest.

A team of guards rushed the room. The lead guy shoved his fingertips into his palm. "Move. Move. Move."

I blew out the incriminating wick and grabbed Wythe's arm, so he wouldn't let me go as the guards encircled us. "We are not done."

"Yet."

That hurt. But it wasn't a total immediate rejection. I'd take it.

We started the slow jog from the room toward the bunker.

He'd have to talk to me now because we were about to be shut into the panic room together. Unless he was horribly put out at how I'd gotten him there. Which he could be.

I would be.

Maybe this was not the best idea. My stomach tightened.

But at least we were together. Maybe this was my best idea. I was fighting for him. Because hiding my emotions hadn't always gotten me what I wanted. Today, I was getting what I wanted. I was fighting for us. Not sitting back and giving up like I did at home. There must have been some point when we were little that I'd just given up and let Felicity get her way because struggling against how unfair being a twin was had rarely gotten me anywhere. I wasn't rolling over today.

We were running now, and my mind was spinning. This run didn't hold the terror or confusion of the first time, and I was trying to get my brain to come up with a solution to this problem. My brain tossed new ideas out with each step. We went through the same corridors, down the same stairs, and then the same door sealed us into the same dark room.

I felt my way to the couch and sank down.

The couch cushion shifted with his weight as he joined me. I didn't look at him, but I could feel his presence, smell the scent of the shower gel he'd used and the lingering cinnamon candle. It was inappropriate and wrong, but I wanted to finish our kiss. To make up with him with a kiss. That's what hit me there in the cinnamon-scented dark. On the couch.

I wanted to kiss him again. Taste him again. Even mad at him. Especially mad at him. I wanted to turn all this inner energy out, to expend it.

The fluorescent lights kicked on, making me blink.

Wythe was beside me, scowling.

Yeah. The darkness hadn't brought out any romantic desires for him. He wasn't totally into this. At least, not yet.

Wythe sat with his legs spread, his hands clasped between

them. "Was this political? Some motive I'm not seeing?"

There was a mood killer. "I don't have an opinion on U.K. politics." I guess maybe I should've, now that I was living here, but I didn't follow them. There were enough to follow back home. With decisions that affected me.

"Must be nice. I don't have that luxury. Opinions shared over dinner affect policy in my family. Words matter. Mistakes matter."

I put my fingertips to my temples and pressed in. That was a complexity of his life I hadn't thought about. I softened. *Oh, Wythe.* I wanted to hug him, shake him, and kiss him all at once. Impossible. Impossible contradictions. I touched his arm, and he tensed under my grip. But he didn't shake me off. "That's kind of empowering, too. Just being here is."

He gave a sharp nod and sank against the backrest, drumming his fingers on the cushion between us. I couldn't read him, but he looked as if he were calculating a math problem in his head. After a minute of that, he turned to face me, his feral blue eyes burning. "Forcing me in here is just not done." He sounded really English.

"I don't give up so easily." I softened my voice, so he wouldn't sense the full intensity of how I felt. "I don't want to."

He blinked and shifted to his feet. "We should talk about class. Our next move." He sounded practical, like he'd asked me to hand him another weight. What an ability to compartmentalize. Must be a British thing, because I didn't have it.

I could only think about us. Our next move. I eyed the couch cushion. We could kiss flat out on the couch. Feed the spark between us.

"For class." His eyes were practical to the point of being cold, and they had the cold shower effect on me. He was fully shutting me out, blanking his face, wearing his public expression.

Great. Yep. Keep it on the inside where we can't fix it, Wythe. Keep it on the inside. Like a Vulcan, a British Vulcan.

My mouth twisted, and I pulled my knees up and in, hugging them. "Wythe." I sounded kind of needy.

"Don't think you'll get out of doing this literature project."

That wasn't what I needed from him. "Wythe."

"Yeah." He nodded, looking almost pleased. "You used me, and I'll use you to finish the class."

He wasn't kicking me out. I had time, and that gave me a chance. That was good. *Calm down. Breathe. He'll get over this. Tell him.* What? What could I say? I shouldn't have sent that photo out. I knew better. I hadn't even read the packet at the time, and I knew better. I could make this up to him.

He got up and paced. "I think we should go to the station."

I wasn't following his meaning. I had to get it together and be useful. Think about class myself before I revealed something I shouldn't reveal. Something about how I felt about him. My heart thumped at the thought, and it caused enough of a jolt of fear that I got my mind in the game. "Why?"

"For the red clue. Paddington Station."

"Okay." I still wasn't fully tracking. Red as a clue could mean the red of Paddington Bear's jacket, or a phone booth, or a random crayon. At the rate of these clues, we wouldn't finish the class before this six-week internship was over.

"This lag between clues…it's so the other teams can catch up? We're going to be in this for a while together." I used the words "we" and "our" deliberately so he'd remember we were in this together.

He shook his head and waved a dismissive hand. "This class is about to spiral into high speed."

"How do you know that?"

He frowned. "The professor's post on the class board. Didn't you read it? Final answers are due by week's end."

I hadn't read that. I shrugged. I really should have read up on the class. But now I knew. I had a week to win him over.

"The professor is not impressed with the class papers or the few guesses that have come in. July's ending. The internship ends in August, too. You and I are almost finished."

We weren't finished. Working on the project would force him to work with me. It gave me time. I clung to that thought. "Did you want to type 'Paddington' in as our answer?"

Wythe shook his head. "Paddington's a central hub. If the new clue requires travel, it'll put us that much closer to wherever we need to go. We'll be ready…if we're not stuck in here." He shot the bunker a resentful look. "The class could end today with a mad rush of clues and me getting stuck with tons of papers because we can't leave this room." He ran his hand over his hair.

I hadn't known most of that. I didn't want to think about it now. Guess that answered my question about graduate school. I wasn't ready to focus on more classwork. I wanted my hands in his hair. *Stop. Shake this off. Concentrate. Don't be so attracted to him. Sound smart. Be smart.* "That would be our ultimate answer then, that a book transports you even when you can't leave the room."

I thought that was a really good answer, but he looked at me like I'd started quoting Shakespeare at him again. He paced. "I should never have agreed to this class."

"The clue could involve Downing Street, and we'd be right here on top of it." I was trying to make my tricking him into coming to this panic room less damaging with that suggestion.

"Not likely."

True. I'd ruled out English writers who'd been politicians. *Okay, focus.* We could get back to…what, a friendship at least? A truce.

I didn't want a truce.

I didn't want to be his friend.

I wanted our clothes on the floor. But I couldn't have that. I had a lot of relationship ground to make up. "Okay. I agree to Paddington Station," I said with a friendly magnanimous tone.

Wythe made a dismissive sound as if I'd commented on the apple-fragranced cleaning product the cleaners had used instead of yielding to his idea. I breathed in and then out. "When exactly is the next clue due to drop?"

"Teatime. The class boards, the ones you didn't read, said we get another clue by teatime. We'd better be out soon." He crossed the room and took clothes from a shelf then went through a small door to the bunker's bathroom.

The sound of water pounding down came through the wall.

A little rude, but it was easier to think without him in the room confusing me. As long as I didn't think about him being in the shower. Unclothed.

Class. Class. Class.

Focus.

I wasn't exactly current with the class or with checking how this puzzle worked. Really, I'd graduated in June. I had nothing left to give academically. Much less enough to be competitive in a high-stress class. But I could help him finish it.

Not just for him. For me. If we didn't come out on top, we'd have to do a lot of papers. I didn't want to write more papers, not this year. But I also didn't want to fail my one and only ever Oxford class. Especially a literature class. A class I had a degree in. That would be horrible, like negating my education or something. I had every reason now to solve the class puzzle. We'd had *King Richard* and now *Red*.

How were they connected?

I pondered it while waiting for Wythe to return and drank a bottle of water from the supplies. I didn't know if there was some sort of bunker supply list I needed to mark, but I figured whoever maintained this place would see the empty plastic water bottle and figure to re-stock. If not, they didn't deserve the position.

Wythe came out, showered, dressed in jeans and a green Henley shirt, rubbing a towel on his wet hair. His skin had to be shower hot and soap scented.

I wanted closer. "I'm thinking about the connection." I had to cough because my voice came out husky. "Richard and Red."

"What a waste. Give me math any day." He narrowed his eyes. "What else have you figured out…and not shared?"

I tilted my head and tried not to react to his jab. He had a right to be put out.

I closed my eyes and thought about the clues. "I figure the answers will be connected. I figure they'll be major English Literature authors. Epic. Historic ones: Austen, Bronte, Chaucer, Dickens... I think we can rule out all former PMs like Churchill and Disraeli. I figure students would complain that it gave you an advantage and say the professor was catering to you and by extension, the ruler of your country."

"They would." Wythe nodded and lost his cold look. He wore a classmate kind of look now. "Go on." He dropped his wet towel on the shelf and found a comb. He dragged it through his towel-dried hair.

I did my best not to stare. Seeing his routine was intimate. I focused on the class. "The professor is a guy, so the ultimate authors he's thinking of are probably men. Unless we have a progressive professor. Then he'll throw in half women, just so he doesn't get called on that BS."

"Narrowing the possibilities. Good."

"Yeah. And, I also ruled out foreigners. If you have enough famous English writers– freaking home of Shakespeare and all, then you don't have to add in the other brilliants who lived here but retained their foreign identity like Oscar Wilde. I mean, Shakespeare. We could blow our ultimate guess on Shakespeare, the Globe, or his home at Stratford on Avon, and not be ashamed. But we really need more clues." My voice picked up enthusiasm. I really did love this topic.

Wythe nodded. "My train station idea is sound. We'll get out of here. Apply my transport advantage to your list, and we'll be at the front. Get this over with."

I nodded with confidence, though all I felt at his words was cold, uncertain, and confined. I kicked off my shoes and lay with my back to the armrest. The couch fabric scratched at my neck. I wedged a throw pillow behind me.

I'd known we had chemistry. I'd known I was crushing on him. I hadn't known how connected we were until it was taken away. We'd get our connection back.

I'd get it back for us.

I had to.

"How close are we to Paddington Station?"

"Not far. It's an advantageous locale. You'll see. With London's traffic, you have to think two steps ahead or you'll end up hours behind." He went on about Westminster in relation to the train station and traffic hours. Before he finished, the door released.

The guard looked in. "All clear." He looked hard at me. "Possibly the candle you were admiring set off our alarm. Though it shouldn't have. We've had the candles removed."

"Great precaution," I said.

The guard snorted.

I stretched, getting off the couch. "So, how many rooms are there like this?"

"I can't say," Wythe said.

"Do you all get your own?"

"It depends on which room we're closest to, and the type of threat. If a route is cut off, we have to go to a backup room."

"Oh." Weird how that sounded somewhat normal.

The guard secured the door behind us. Wythe and I took the stairs up to the main entry.

"I met your brother." There. That was casual friendly conversation.

He sent me a sharp glance. "Why would you want to meet Zane?"

"Why wouldn't I? Is he like you or Caroline?" *Tell me about yourself.*

He frowned. "He's himself. And, like me, so over the manipulation." He wasn't making a dig, just stating a fact.

A whirring sounded, and the door opened, freeing us from one chamber to the next. Then we were out of security and outside in the mild English summer. We stood on the curb, waiting for the car.

"Wythe. I don't want to be one of the people in your life who manipulates you."

"Really, Kira. Don't." Wythe faced forward. "Because, you know, and I know, you already are."

The black town car pulled up and he got in, leaving me standing there.

It hurt.

My insides hurt. The breaths hurt. Why? Anger at my sister? Embarrassment? Oh, no.

It really was my heart.

The worst kind of hurt.

Chapter 15

Act normal and things would go back to normal. That's how I handled fallouts with my sister. I pretended she hadn't royally pissed me off. She pretended none of my digs pissed her off, and we moved on. Often with a small silent treatment, which was what Felicity was getting now from me. Felicity was used to it.

Wythe didn't just give me the silent treatment. He played cold and distant. A British specialty. Not one word in the car on the way to Paddington Station.

We pulled up right beside a brass statue of Paddington Bear. Tourists were posing with him. "Let's get savory pastries and pose with that bear."

I could see him warring with his hunger. Wythe pushed out his lip. "It *is* teatime."

There really was no set teatime. Teatime meant afternoon snack and could happen any time after lunch and before dinner. I wanted a pasty. The half-moon shaped potpies were a much more travel-friendly shape than our own little pies because I could eat the half-moons without a fork and they could be carried in my hand. An eco-friendly kind of takeout. "I want a potato-cheese one."

Interest sparked in Wythe's eyes. "They may still have steak ones."

I paused at the bear on the way in, waiting for the tourists to finish their snapshot. I was getting a selfie. Sure, I could have ignored the whole selfie sore point. But then, things around it would fester. I was ripping the band-aid off on the photo issue. Wythe was looking around as if he wasn't used to the train station.

"Wythe. Come here."

He looked at me like I was crazy.

"Get in the photo with me. If 'Paddington' is correct, great, we'll get a tick mark. But if he's not, at least we can send in this picture with Paddington wearing his little red jacket, and the Professor will understand why we thought of 'red' and bear books." I was overexplaining to persuade him.

He wavered. More than one tourist was waiting for me to move so they could get their shot. I wasn't budging. That, more than anything, made him lean in and pose.

Then we entered the train station. Paddington Station smelled of London air and train exhaust and held a ton of commuters all going purposefully in different directions. Two couples rolled bags along the colored floor stickers leading them to the Heathrow Express. A group of guys in soccer jerseys headed to the underground entrance. A guy in a striped suit carrying a briefcase strode toward the taxi queue. A few were like me and Wythe, less purposeful.

Stores and restaurants enclosed the railway tracks on one end. We got our food at a kiosk and found an iron bench. After the first cheesy bite and sip of semi-warm fizzy soda, my phone pinged with an incoming email. I clicked on it, hoping for the next clue. Something Wythe and I could talk about.

The email was from Felicity. I opened it. *Waking up to another glorious day. Going to hit the Smithsonian for some sight-seeing. Or is it site-seeing? Whichever. D.C. in the summer is such a treat. Are you getting any touring in? I know I'm lucky to be so ahead on my assignments. Is it raining there? Again. Don't let those wet plop-plops stop you from getting out.*

Whatever. She didn't even mention what she had done. Brat.

I started to reply but another email popped up, saving me from breaking my silence. This one was from the professor. *Wythe and Kira are in the lead. First, with their King Richard solve. Now with a creative take on "red."*

Nice. I tapped Wythe's arm so he'd lean in and read with me. *May the other teams strive to match their superior progress as we speed to the end of term. I expect a paper on King Richard from the rest of class for failing to guess Shakespeare first. Really, lads. The progress toward solving my literary puzzle has been less than stellar. In the words of Ian Fleming, "Never say no to adventures. Always say yes. Otherwise, you'll lead a very dull life."*

The thrill of a win made me grin at Wythe. I waved my pasty and my soda in a small circle, Felicity forgotten. "Ha."

His eyes glinted, but he didn't say anything.

My phone blinked with an incoming video chat invite. Names appeared: *Vihaan Laghari and Peppa.* I accepted the chat and a window opened. Vihaan and Peppa stared back at us. Vihaan was as dark as Peppa was fair. I hadn't seen him before, but his identity was a safe bet because Wythe had said they were partners.

Behind them was a black lion statue. They were at Trafalgar Square. Vihaan leaned into the camera. "Live big for now, team one. But remember we are doing well also. First place." Vihaan's voice became strangled. "Is this the doing of your new partner?" He turned to Peppa. "Did you know of her, Peppa?"

Peppa inclined her head. "Of course." But her brow wrinkled. I didn't know if she had known. I hadn't told her.

"How did you get a girl on your team? We haven't seen her." Vihaan clicked on his phone instead of waiting for me to answer. "Did you transfer? How come we don't know you?"

I leaned in closer. "Hi."

Peppa narrowed her gray eyes. Vihaan widened his dark brown ones.

"Live small, team two. You're about to lose again." I drawled out the words.

Vihaan said, "She is American. Wythe, you joined forces with an American on a British literature quest?" Vihaan laughed, and his words came out garbled. "Well done, mate, that'll get you far." He'd gone from speaking as if I were a threat to dismissing me.

I didn't like it.

"I'm sure your team will do better next go around," Wythe said, sounding like he wasn't sure they would.

Peppa pushed Vihaan's shoulder. "Move in. They can see where we are."

Vihaan leaned even closer to the camera, sending the lens up one of his nostrils. "When will we be meeting with Kira?" He sounded eager. There must not have been that many women in the class.

"She's busy," Wythe said.

Vihaan shook his head. "But as the only two teams in the top, we should get together and share notes. Have a cup of tea."

Peppa was facing her partner, her profile to us. There had to be a phrase for that. *Giving us the side-face* didn't cover it. Peppa said, "You heard she's American, right? Doesn't that establish that she doesn't drink tea? She's staying with us at Downing Street. Can you believe it?"

She said "Downing Street" like the place was holy, like she owned it.

"Yep. Downing Street. A place built on a Middle Ages brewery." I'd read my packet and my *UK Telegraph*. "Named after Sir George Downing. Educated at Harvard. You know, in America."

Peppa frowned as I yanked her chain.

"How about the pub then?" Vihaan asked.

I nodded. "I haven't been to an English pub." I shook my head at Wythe, so he'd know I was lying. "Sounds fun."

Their heads jerked back in incomprehension.

"We'll do that then," Wythe said.

"We'll do that then," Peppa echoed and turned back to us, her eyes so narrow now they were almost closed. "How about now? Where are you? Are those trains?"

Wythe clicked the screen off. "We'll text you."

Chapter 16

We entered the crowded pub. Wythe looked around and said, "Downstairs."

I followed him, weaving through the small tables. "I thought we were meeting them at a pub with a Goat in the name, not a Cheese in the name."

Wythe entered the stairwell. He was bent at the waist, barely making it down the low dark stairs ahead of me. "Did I say that?"

"Yeah. You did." I was glad the other two wouldn't be joining us, but I wanted to know his reasoning. The steps were steep and awkward; I grabbed the handrail. They took us into a drinking cellar, and we found a corner table. I sank into the dark wooden chair. Music played down here, classic British pop tunes. At home, they'd play Top 40 music. Here they stuck to the proven.

Wythe shrugged. "They'll go to a goat pub. We'll go here." He looked around at the Ye Olde Cheshire Cheese built in 1667. "I thought you'd like it. Dickens and Twain drank here."

I did like that. I liked it even more that he thought to pick a pub that would appeal to me. "'It was the best of times, it was the worst of times.' Charles Dickens. It fits my summer."

The corner of Wythe's mouth quirked. It made me want to think of more quotes. Quotes to toast to in this pub with its darkened lighting, low ceilings, and massive bar. Mom would have called this place a traditional proper pub. I didn't know what she'd think about me being out with Wythe. She'd probably worry. But she would like that security accompanied me. "Your guards won't come in?"

"They're here somewhere. Sometimes, they're good at achieving discretion. Other times less so." He seemed resigned and used to it. How long had that taken? I wanted to ask, but it seemed almost a tabloid-type question: Tell us, Wythe, how the son of the Prime Minister really feels about his protection detail.

I sipped my apple cider. It tasted like bitter apple juice with an alcoholic kick. I'd have preferred a mixed drink where I couldn't taste the alcohol, but there was nothing on the menu with a drink name I recognized, and nothing that looked like it came with a paper umbrella or cherry on top.

Wythe drank a dark ale. A guy in a pub. Me here with him. It felt like a date. I snapped a photo of our tabletop, making sure to get my hand in the shot but not him. I showed him the picture and sent it off to a friend back in Texas. My friends weren't getting the brush-off, just Felicity. *#AtaPubwithaFriend.* I held in the snicker. *#HighStoolWeather.* That's what they called rainy days here.

"Writing your sister?"

"She's getting the silent treatment." I turned my phone,

so he could read my message. "She's my fraternal twin. Evil, unlike your siblings. Caroline's a kick. I see her around. Why haven't I seen Zane much?"

"Zane's not as patient as I am when it comes to all this." He gestured around the bar.

Like he was patient. "Beer and pubs?"

Wythe wore a small frown. "Guards and expectations. They get old. Beer and pubs? Zane likes those." He seemed less angry.

I had to ask him if he meant what he'd said. "Speaking of...are you really not going to any more charity events? Not even one?" I peeled at the corner of the label on my bottle, tearing off the stem to the apple. All I needed was one more point. My tone was casual, but my heart thumped hard as I waited for his reply.

He tilted his head. "I might."

"If?"

"For the right incentive."

I knew he didn't mean a kiss. He was still too upset with me. "Such as my helping you with this class?" Which I'd already agreed to do.

Wythe waved that off. "Your grade is the reward."

"We don't seem to be getting graded."

"We'll get a grade at the end."

"In the U.S., we get regular graded tests and papers. You know where you stand." Though we were probably thinking about literature now more than if we'd studied for a test and then forgotten what we'd written as soon as we turned it in. "Why are you even taking another class? I read the packet, and you've graduated. I hadn't realized that."

He sighed. "I can't easily take a job. Not in my field. Civil engineering contracts come from the government."

It would look like a civil engineering firm gave him a job in exchange for winning a government contract. He'd been trapped by his mom's success. There was probably something Freudian I could say about that, but I couldn't think of anything offhand.

"I was kind of forced to take this internship. There was a lot of family pressure. And a lot of helpful advisors saying it would be great for my resume. I couldn't get out of it. But your pressures..." I gestured to the entry with my glass. "Your family challenges put mine in perspective." I put my glass down and threw my arms back. "I'm free." I may have extended the "e" a bit long, because he chuckled. Which was good. I poured the last of the cider into my glass and went back to toying with the bottle. "How did you end up in a lit class?"

"I told my parents I'd delay a job while Mom's in office. She has enough pressure. I told her I wanted to take another class." He scowled. "Peppa was sorting it, hounding me for a response, so I told her I didn't give a..." He paused without cursing. "To sign me up for anything."

I finished for him. "So, she put you in her own class." It made total sense to me. I might have done the same thing if given the opportunity.

Wythe nodded. "I committed to taking a class. So, I'll finish it." His drink had mellowed him. "What would you be asking me if we'd just met for the first time?"

I tilted my head, mirroring his motion. "Well. In Texas, we'd be at a party. Your beer would be in a red plastic cup, that at some point you'd squeeze too hard, so it would spill. Or I would spill mine. It would give the whole place a light beer smell. Not unlike this bar. Also, there'd be fewer soccer jerseys than here, and more t-shirts. And some guy would be walking around carrying a bag of wine. You'd slap the bag if you wanted some."

He leaned forward. "Yes?"

"Yep." I made myself sound super enthused about "slap the bag." Though wine wasn't my favorite drink. I preferred this cider.

He leaned back and laughed, sounding free, and looking younger, and so attractive. If I had seen him across a party… Whew. I would've been the first over to meet him. Not that I would've been obvious about it. I'd have gotten near and given him *the look*, and watched to see if it worked. If it hadn't, I'd have had to pull out other tricks.

I clicked my glass to his bottle. "'Bring in the bottled lightning, a clean tumbler, and a corkscrew.' Dickens."

He arched a brow. "Dickens? Really?"

"Dickens. Really. A great quote. But not my favorite." I winked at him.

He arched both eyebrows. "Is it, 'More, please?'"

I grinned. "Yeah, that's good." I waved my empty bottle. "More, please."

He brought me another drink.

I took a sip, apple with a kick. This one was somehow even better. "No, we're off Dickens." I toyed with a paper coaster that advertised a German beer. "So many great drinking quotes. You've never truly toasted until you've drunk with a Lit major."

"Give me one then."

"'I solemnly swear that I am up to no good.'"

He tapped my glass and took a long pull from his drink.

135

"I must say, living literature is much better than reading it."

I was in turns defensive of literature and in love with his phrase. I chose to go with the love. "Living literature. Love it. Some version of that would make a good 'ultimate' guess for class."

"Maybe." He grinned. "Not familiar with the 'no good' quote. Courtroom book?"

I snickered. "*Harry Potter*."

"I'm a fan."

"I'd hope so. *Harry Potter* is a national treasure. Which leads me to a question for you." I was eager for this one, and I leaned in.

Wythe kicked his feet out. "Okay."

"Why don't we go see the *Harry Potter* play?" A couple of ciders in, and I was asking him out. Yep. Heat flushed my cheeks, well, heat and the warm room, but I didn't take the offer back.

He blinked and sat up straighter. His eyes searched mine. "I'll go if it's off the books. You and me."

I loved that. A smile curled my lips. An inappropriate smile, given that fraternization wasn't allowed. I didn't care. He'd just turned my proposition officially into a date. An unspoken date, an unsaid date, but a date nonetheless. This way, if questioned, I could say I hadn't dated him. If the interrogator went into kissing... Well, then, I'd have to plead the fifth. Did they have the fifth amendment here? Or was it all guilty first and self-incrimination and ship her off to the Colonies? I didn't know, and I wasn't keen to find out. But I was eager to go with him. Me. Him. Him and me. London theatre. The dark. "Okay."

His eyes grew heated.

I wanted to pursue that.

Ping.

Both our phones went off. Email. It was from the lit professor. "Clue: super American steak." The clues were coming faster.

"This one's all you," Wythe said, his voice teasing and challenging. "What's an American steak?"

I thought about the first clue, that flash of red. "Super. Super. Superman, Supersize. Superduper." I sounded slightly tipsy. I'd order a water next.

"Okay, super, and what's an American steak?"

"I don't know…T-bone, sirloin, chopped beef."

He ran through probabilities with those. I closed my eyes and thought of England. Red, white, and blue on both their flags. Steak. Steak. Steak. I had nothing.

"What are you doing?"

"I'm closing my eyes and thinking of England." It was an old joke about how one tolerated bad sex.

Wythe choked out a laughed. "Is that what you do?" He put his drink down and looked really interested. "Does it work?"

"I wouldn't know." Yep, the cider made me put it out there. I hadn't gone there with my ex. Almost. But nope.

"You haven't had bad sex?" He hadn't lost his intrigued expression. If anything, I was fueling it.

This was the point in the conversation where I would change the subject if I had no interest in him. I didn't change the subject. "I haven't had sex-sex." I wasn't inexperienced, but I hadn't gone all the way there.

He rolled his pint glass between his palms and didn't break eye contact with me. His blue eyes glinted. "You wouldn't have to think of England with me...or close your eyes."

I swallowed and closed my eyes again. Partly to stop how much his gaze and words were turning me on. I was soft enough around him. No guy liked an easy catch.

"What are you doing now?" Wythe sounded challenged, like I was the puzzle.

"I'm closing my eyes and thinking of America. And steak." And I made myself do it. Dinner, Angus beef, Nolan Ryan beef, Kobe beef. Those were choices at home. They even had steak at the dorm cafe. A chopped beef patty with brown gravy and a single spongy mushroom floating in the sauce every week. There was something there. "On the school lunch menu, we had Salisbury steak. It was disgusting."

"That's what you think of English food?" He shook his head. "We don't have that."

I Googled it. "It's named after a New York doctor... but...York. Back to the King Richard reference. I bet it's right."

Wythe tapped his fingers on the table. "We do not have Salisbury steak, but we do have a Salisbury. Salisbury has a cathedral, and it's known for its connection to Richard III."

We spit out random theories, each growing wilder and bigger as we finished our drinks.

I dropped my forehead to the table and wanted to pound it. "Salisbury..."

"Salisbury Plain has Stonehenge," he said, sounding even more into this.

He was so right. "Yes! What's England without Stonehenge? Stonehenge. How far?" I pulled up my phone's map app. "We can Google it."

"We have a car. Want to go there in the morning?"

That moment was fantastical. We were in sync, and in this crazy country. We could drive to Stonehenge. How amazing was that? I looked into his eyes. "Yes."

There was a pause in the night, and then the music changed to one of those songs everyone knew. As if they'd been trained, the pub crowd started singing, including Wythe. It was such a European guy thing to do I just stared at him. He smiled at me, and it was so tempting to keep him smiling that I found myself singing, too.

It was a great night at the pub.

***

The day was gorgeous, and Wythe shrugged out of his jacket on the way to the car. He wore a gray t-shirt over a long-sleeve t-shirt. English weather required layers. I wore a cream t-shirt under a rust-colored jacket. We both wore jeans and hiking shoes. We were headed to the countryside.

Wythe wasn't as easygoing this morning as he had been after a glass of ale. His armor was back up. I didn't want any awkward silences, so I Googled facts on the drive and read more about the Neolithic period and the eighty-three stones than I'd ever wanted to know. It wasn't until Wythe Googled *super* and *Stonehenge* that we got our answer. In 2015, they discovered a new hidden circle of stones surrounding the existing monument. They called it Superhenge.

"I still don't get how 'red' fits in," I said.

"It's enough. We'll type it and send it off to the professor." Wythe sounded eager to get our outing over with.

That bummed me. I held up my hand to slow him down. "What's this have to do with lit?"

He shrugged. "We'll figure a connection out later."

At least he'd said "we."

Moving together, we trudged up the gravel path, looking for the answer. Rolling hills surrounded us, and the air was chillier here outside of London. Ten minutes in, invigorated by all the clean air, I thought to take a shot at the real question hovering over us. *Can we be friends again? Something more?* I looked at him.

He faced straight ahead. No more little looks at me. Not angry. Just not interested or happy with me. He was right there. But not there. Not really. And I missed him. "Since this place is all supernatural…"

"Is it?" he asked.

"Yeah. Can we play time travel? Pretend, just for today, that the whole PR thing didn't happen?"

Chapter 17

He stiffened, and his footsteps sounded heavier on the crunchy path. I could see the big fat disappointing "no" coming my way.

I wanted to offer to give up on the internship and its point system. But it would be like letting Felicity win and I couldn't do that. He mattered though, and that left me conflicted.

I was only clear about today. I wanted it. "Not forever, just today. Let's have a solid truce until we get back to Westminster and the real world."

Wythe looked down at me, his wild blue eyes flashing. What I'd said clearly appealed to him. He gave a sharp nod.

Relief and pleasure lit into me, showing me how much his response meant to me.

We reached the ropes that encircled the rings, and I grinned big, using the stones as the excuse for my smile. "This place is crazy amazing. When I came with my family, it was packed. We'd had to stand in line for twenty minutes at the visitor center for ice cream."

"Give it a minute," Wythe said. "I'm sure a tour bus or two holding sixty people each will be by soon. But for now, what we have here is an opportunity." Wythe grabbed the nearest rope. Breaking the cardinal rule of ropes, he lifted it.

What? A weird rush went through me. "We can't go under the ropes. They'll deport me or something." I looked around, sure an immigration agent was about to pop up from behind a stone. No one came running. Random groups of tourists and locals with dogs wandered around the path and out in the fields, but no one went closer to the stones. Everyone obeyed the ropes.

"Oh, but we can." He sounded teasing and confident.

"We can't."

Wythe looked entitled. "We're not going to damage the rocks."

"The ropes are here for a reason. To protect this archeological site from people like us."

"The ropes are here to protect the site from people who'd chip off pieces of the stones for a souvenir. That's not us."

"We have something similar in Texas. You can't pick the bluebonnet flowers."

"Flowers regrow."

"A national treasure is a national treasure."

"It's a flower, and Texas isn't a nation."

"It was once. We had an embassy in central London."

Wythe ignored my words. He wiggled the rope and arched his eyebrow at me in invitation.

I couldn't resist that. I slipped under, feeling an illicit thrill.

We crossed the grass to the interior stones, with our heads up high as if we belonged there. We were standing where no one was supposed to be standing. Like ancient druids instead of naughty tourists. I looked around. "I like it. But what are we doing in here?" I grabbed his hand. In for a penny, in for a pound.

He led me farther in, behind a big rock. "For this." He pressed me against the stone, leaned down, and kissed me.

Soft. Warm. His kiss was everything that was right with the world. My lips tingled and parted.

He kissed me lightly, and then firmly, with conviction, as if this was the only place he wanted to be.

I pressed against him, and he pressed me back. The rough stone behind me and the cool air contrasted with the heat we were generating. It made the feelings more intense. Or maybe it was the arguing. Or maybe there was some mystical force at work. But I felt like a lit cinnamon candle.

I tightened my arms around his neck.

He ran his hands down my back and up again, sharing more supernatural kisses with me. It was unlike anything I'd ever felt and like everything I'd ever wanted. What had been wrong with kisses before? None had had this feeling of joining, this connection.

I shivered and rubbed against him.

He murmured something I didn't understand. His mouth moved to my neck, sending sparks there.

"Wythe." His name came out half murmur, half gasp. I wanted him to lay me down, right there in the middle of those stones. Like an ancient offering. A ritual. A merging. Two souls. Two bodies. His. Mine.

"*Oi.*" A guy in a Stonehenge slicker jerked his thumb toward the path. "You two."

The interruption was awful, jolting me out of something

amazing. I made a frustrated growl, but a ladylike one.

Wythe pulled back and grinned at me. A crooked grin, a wicked grin.

I loved it, and it made the frustration okay. Because we shared it. We left the inner ring, hands interlaced, and stepped back onto the crunchy path.

There was no other correction from the park guard. He was satisfied that we'd listened, and he'd moved on down the crunchy path.

Stonehenge. It was just stones and a hill. But there was something magical there. Something about seeing a structure I'd seen my whole life, being there in person…being there with Wythe was amazing.

I wanted him to feel wonderful, too. I wanted to give him something. Solve this puzzle for him. "Is there a Sci-Fi book featuring Stonehenge? Have you read any books set in the rings? Or, what's old and epic like the rings? Old. Old English. Beowulf maybe?"

He looked blank.

I waved my free hand as I thought aloud. "Old. England's old epic poem."

He shrugged, and then he shook his head. "Nah. This is prehistoric, not old English."

"Celts. Romans." I released him and searched online for more random info about the monument. "Chaucer. Mallory. Tenneson."

He shook his head. "I think we should be more literal. Quotes about Stonehenge maybe?"

I Googled one. "'The immemorial gray pillars may serve to remind you of the enormous background of time.' Henry James, an American. I rather like that."

"But he's American."

I searched further. "American who attained British citizenship. I think that's qualification enough. Let's go with him."

We took a selfie with Stonehenge in the distance. I sent it in along with the quote. "This shows we were actually here." I didn't think Wythe believed I'd upload the photo onto a blog, not anymore, but I was being cautious, which was why I explained the picture.

We wandered back along the dirt road, which felt like a very English dirt road compared to my American pastures. Something about the temperature or the quality of the sun and air. I pointed down the stretch. "My favorite quote is by J.R.R. Tolkien. Born in South Africa, but an English writer, professor."

"Don't make me yawn."

I nudged him with my shoulder. "'Not all those who wander are lost.'"

Wythe nodded. "I like that. Origin?"

"*The Lord of the Rings.*"

He Googled it. "'All that is gold does not glitter, not all those who wander are lost; the old that is strong does not wither, deep roots are not reached by the frost.'" He swiped his fingers across the screen. "'Still 'round the corner there may wait, a new road or a secret gate.' Tolkien." He grinned, looking carefree. "I won't be reading it." He dropped his arm over my shoulders. "I'll send those in, too, though. Maybe we'll get a bonus." He pulled me in for a selfie, getting the curve of the road behind us.

When he snapped the picture, I turned into his chest for a moment, resting my forehead against the gray cotton of his shirt, feeling my hair whip around us in the breeze. I reached up a hand and touched the black cord he wore at his neck. He looked so relaxed today. Just a guy. Not like the PM's son. Just a guy. Here with me. I knew what was behind my interest in these pictures, and it was more than to add value to a class project. To make us real to a digital-age professor. It was to have pictures of us. For me.

This moment was important. My heart felt it. I hoped his did, too. I looked into his eyes. He looked into mine. We had our connection back. He gave me a quick melting kiss and then we turned to go back down the path.

A duo was on the road coming our way.

Westminster had come to us. Peppa and Vihaan. Wythe stepped farther away from me, which I hated. But discretion was the better part of finishing this internship.

On the plus side, if they'd chosen Stonehenge, too, it was further evidence that we'd guessed the clue correctly.

Peppa reached forward and held out her hand to Wythe. He shook it, but in that restrained British way, as if startled by the touching and not terribly eager for it.

"We missed you at the pub yesterday," Peppa said.

I smiled at her. "Must have been a miscommunication."

Peppa didn't like that, and her expression was one that I hated seeing in other women. A "girls competing over a guy" kind of expression. So stupid. He liked you or he didn't. Yearning, bitchy looks wouldn't alter it. Or maybe this was about the internship.

"I'm Vihaan." Vihaan looked at me under his heavy eyelids. It was an attempted come-on. After what he'd done ot Wythe, did he think I'd be interested in him? Annoyance flickered through me. Selling his classmate out. Not cool.

Not at all like what I'd done. The thought of my own mistake made guilt churn in my stomach.

Peppa looked at the rings in the distance. "What was your answer? Have you sent in your ultimate guess? Vihaan and I are almost ready."

I didn't believe her. "We'll never tell." I used it as an excuse to wave and keep walking.

***

Back in the town car, the privacy glass gave us the illusion of being alone together. Me and Wythe. I planned to pretty much stare at him the whole drive back.

He was good-looking, fit, intelligent... *Stop drooling over him.* I'd read that handsome men made selfish lovers. They lay back for the woman to do all the work. I wouldn't know about that, but this guy *was* spoiled.

I could do some of the work.

Heat hit my face. *Stop.*

Selfish equaled bad in bed. He was bad in bed.

I looked him over again. Shoulders built to hold onto. A waist narrow enough to wrap my legs around. *Stop.*

Handsome.

Bad in bed.

But what if he wasn't? I'd done a lot in college, but I hadn't done that. I'd never felt for another guy what I felt for him.

The flush of chemistry that rolled over me made me suck in a breath. Or maybe it was the thoughts that stole my breath. Why? In preparation for a kiss. I had to get out of here before I jumped him. I turned my attention to the countryside and my phone, splitting the time.

The car had reached the road along the Thames now. It calmed and disappointed me at the same time. We were nearing Westminster. Our truce was almost over.

The car went through the security gates. I could walk from here. I reached for the door handle.

"Wait," Wythe said.

I dropped my hand and turned to him as if he were the sun and I was Venus.

"What's that expression?" Wythe sounded intellectually curious.

The tone cooled me down.

Some.

He tilted his head at a confident angle. "Thinking about me?"

So much. Heat flushed my face. "Sort of."

He grinned. A cocky guy grin. One that said he knew I'd been performing mental naughtiness with him as the star. "Yeah. I'm all that."

I had to shut that down or end up under his heel like the gum splotches that marred the sidewalks. "I was thinking earlier how they say handsome guys are bad in bed."

He straightened, and his face stilled.

"And you're really handsome." I dug it in further. "Really handsome."

A flush hit his cheeks. He didn't laugh, as I'd half intended. Or shake it off. He leaned forward, cupped my cheek, and put his mouth to my ear.

I shivered. He hadn't even done or said anything, and I'd quivered in anticipation. Yep, that was me.

"Anytime." The word, said in his deep voice, was an offer.

I trembled harder, making my face brush his. Oh, my. I shook.

"Anytime," he whispered again, "you want to test that theory, I'm willing to prove it wrong.

My breath caught.

He got out of the car, leaving me sitting there like a puddle of goo. I know. I know. Guys could do it without the emotion. But I couldn't. I couldn't take him up on his "anytime." It'd be physical but emotionless. I couldn't fake that kind of detachment. Not after I'd felt something real between us…something I couldn't name, but something real…something sex wouldn't bring back.

***

I focused on class in a way I hadn't before. If I could get this right for him, it would mean something to me. My thoughts came together the next day during the hour Wythe went jogging. I put on my running gear and went outside to the path that wove through the rose bushes. I took the path at a slow jog, looking out for him.

Wythe was up ahead, bent forward, hands on his knees, the way runners caught their breath after they pushed themselves. Poised there, with the hedges behind him, hair sweat-dampened, he was an ad for British summers. He turned his head toward me. "Hey."

Even his freaking greetings pleased me. I was crazy. I went up to him. "Got some new ideas for class."

"Go ahead." He didn't sound super intrigued.

I had to work harder. The trail crunched under our feet as we headed back to the security entrance. "Put them all together. King Richard and Salisbury led us to Stonehenge. Stonehenge led us to …"

"I got nothing."

He wasn't trying enough, and I wasn't just giving it up. "What was Stonehenge's purpose?"

"To give us an engineering puzzle. A history mystery."

Better. "Sort of. The answer is we don't know. Temple. Meeting Place. Court. Auditorium. We don't know. So, King Richard. And something we don't know...like..." I went with the big obvious in an English lit author puzzle. "Shakespeare." I said the name with the reverence it deserved. "He's a massive British mystery. Was the guy really the author of all those works? Or, was he covering for someone else? Like the queen? It's really fascinating, right?"

"Okay," he said, but he didn't seem that interested, just mildy amused by my enthusiasm. "Go on."

"I thought Stratford, where he's from, but time's winding down. Sending us to the countryside to dig up more clues isn't practical." Though what was practical for the average Oxford student might differ from practicality for the average broke co-ed. Besides, this had kind of jumped out at me. "No one knows if he was one or many authors. But we know there's a King Richard play. We know the Stonehenge rings are circular." I made a circle with my fingers. "So circular Shakespeare and London...that can only be..."

He stared at me blankly.

He'd so fail without me. My mouth twitched. "Shakespeare's Theatre—the Globe. We can go there."

Wythe touched a finger to the side of his temple. "Got it. Let me hit the shower. Meet me at the front in twenty."

"Make it thirty." I wasn't wearing gym clothes to the Globe.

***

We headed to the Globe, the famous re-creation of the theatre that had staged Shakespeare's plays. I had on a sleeveless peach floral top, a floaty delicate one, with Capri jeans and sandals. I'd worn my hair down and applied light makeup. It was one of those looks that screamed casual but had taken me the full half hour to put together—and that was with me rushing.

Wythe didn't say anything about my outfit, but he did give me more than one once-over, especially my hair. I had to stop with the ponytails.

He tapped his fingertips together. "These clues aren't that obscure, once you add a literature degree to the mix." He'd given me a compliment.

I melted some at the evidence of his thawing. "I kind of think the professor wants many interpretations more than a definitive answer. To see how we think. *If* we think."

"Yeah." He purchased tickets, mentioning we were here for a class.

"Nice." The female cashier unclipped her hair and fluffed it. "You can go in now. No need to queue."

"What about the line?" I pointed at tourists on benches, obviously waiting, clearly ahead of us.

The cashier only had eyes for Wythe. "You have a special time," the cashier said. "Better access." She either recognized him as the PM's son or she thought he was hot. She handed him two brochures that looked like scripts and listed the summer play production schedule.

We went in.

I'd been here as a kid with my family, but it awed me

even more now. Wooden stadium seats faced the empty stage. Shakespeare. I'm not saying this place was an English lit major's dream come true. But it was close.

Wythe checked out the structure. "Green oak, thatched roof based on reeds they found during the excavation."

"So, what's your favorite Shakespeare quote? Let me guess." I bounced up and down. Being here was such a thrill, it sent a rush through me. Being here with him made it even better. The breeze stirred over me. A quote that fit him, and this situation, was easy. "'All the world's a stage, and all the men and women merely players.'"

"So much literature." He looked slightly hunted.

"Yep." And it was awesome. This place was breathtaking. When I'd been here before, the rows had been packed with timed entrants. Right now, we were the only people here. That cashier had definitely given Wythe special treatment. I didn't blame her.

"We'll send your quote in." Wythe went to the edge of the stage and gave me a boost before climbing up. He was either entitled or simply knew which rules were silly.

I still had to protest. "We're not supposed to be…"

He winked, clearly in a fun mood, and that shut me up. "'All the world's a stage, and all the men and women merely players.'" He held out his hand. "Play with me?"

Oh. Yes. I took his hand.

"Ready for your stage kiss?"

Chapter 18

Yeah. I was ready for my stage kiss. I tilted my head to make him work for it. "Send in our quote first, kind sir, because I doth think thou must earn it."

Wythe grinned and typed it in as we stood there on the stage of stages, saying the words aloud at the same time. "'All the world's a stage...'" Wythe hit send and then pulled me to him the way actors had done on stage for centuries, with a dramatic swoop. And he kissed me. It differed from the mystical Stonehenge kiss with the cool breeze from the plains. This kiss had the energy of the theatre. The thrill of ghostly onlookers. The promise of praise.

Then the kiss turned. We weren't playing anymore. My brain grew fuzzy. And I felt the moment. It was him and me. Us. Warmth. Energy. Electricity. Fire.

Someone cleared her throat. This was no ghost of an audience long past. This was now.

Peppa and Vihaan.

Peppa was glaring up at us with her hands crossed over her chest. Vihaan looked like he wanted to give us a thumbs-up.

She'd busted us. She was the head intern. She knew about the "no touching" rule.

"It's for the clue." I brushed my hands over my shirt and jeans as if they were in disarray. "*Romeo and Juliet.*" I could have kicked myself. Excuses and fidgeting screamed guilt.

"She's not interning right now, Peppa. Lose the look," Wythe said.

Peppa shrugged. "I'm just upset you beat us here. That's all."

"Barely." Vihaan glared beside her, hands splayed. "They are only moments ahead of us." He cocked his head back, looking up at us. "Getting a bit close for comfort now, isn't it?" He was talking about the competition, not my internship.

They *were* weirdly right behind us on this quest. I guess the clue had been an easy one because we'd come up with the answer at almost the same time as them. The other teams would probably be barging in any moment. Were we slipping from our number one spot? I wouldn't let them know they'd worried me. "Close only counts in horseshoes," I said, giving Vihaan one of Felicity's favorite taunts.

Vihaan's blank expression implied horseshoes might not be such a known game over here.

Wythe and I needed to get away from them to brainstorm our next step. I backed up. A groove had been notched out of the stage floor. Stage actors needed a swift getaway. I lifted it. Stairs. I climbed in. The ladder chute smelled like costumes, hairspray, and makeup. We were in the actors' area for sure. "Come on, Wythe."

He was right behind me as I went down the black wooden stairs. But when I reached the last rung, the stairs just stopped, hanging well above the floor. A giant cushion underneath served as a landing. I crossed my fingers and let go.

Whoosh.

The air left my body but in a rushed way, not a starved-of-oxygen way.

Wythe landed on my left.

I knew he would. He wasn't the type of guy to crawl back up and circle around rather than take the plunge.

He rolled beside me and turned on his side. The move rotated my body toward his. His gaze examined me in a deep pensive way.

I didn't move. I was stuck there like an actress who'd forgotten her line. Like an ancient stargazer enamoured of the sky. Like an intern falling for the hot Prime Minister's son.

He threaded his fingers through my hair, his expression curious and then almost sad. "There's a maritime lecture Thursday afternoon in Greenwich. We should go."

That was the last day I could get an intern point. "Would that get me a point?"

He looked at me like I'd said the wrong thing, rolled away, and got up.

I wanted to call him back. Instead, I watched him walk away. At that moment, I knew I'd rather have him here with me, even if it meant I failed the internship. The win against Felicity was no longer enough; I wanted more out of this summer.

***

I wasn't ready yet to give up on the internship photo, and I had a plan. Tomorrow was Thursday, the last possible day for an internship. If I solved the class puzzle, Wythe would be so grateful that he'd agree to an internship point event tomorrow. I caught up to Wythe in the gym. I could have waited until he finished his workout, but why would I? Seeing his muscles bunch and release as he went through the machines was a treat.

He knew I was watching, but he didn't stop. Even in a white t-shirt and navy sweats, he looked great. I'd buy a gym membership from him.

"Kira," he said as he wiped his face with a towel when he'd finished on the bench press.

I liked his tone. It was as if the truce we'd created had held. *Kira.* I liked my name in his accent. I wanted to hear it again.

He arched his eyebrow when I said nothing. "Kira?" He stretched out his arms and legs and leaned forward.

I had to answer him. My excuse to be here was a new email from the professor. This class was the weirdest. Classes back home had rarely bucked the traditional lecture and multiple-choice test model. Sometimes. But rarely. "We got a new email from class." I waved my phone. "'Your mission, should you choose to accept it, deliver this clue'"—I made quotes—"'to the team you believe will come after you. Give them a relevant author name.'"

The task was mean, like in those reality shows where they made the contestants name who should go home. I always thought those episodes were especially vicious. In our case, it was easy though. We hadn't seen anyone else from class other than Vihaan and Peppa. They were the team in second place.

"Vihaan and Peppa," Wythe said.

"Exactly. So, we need to give them an author name."

"Any author?" Wythe raised his eyebrows. "That's my level of literary gameplay. I can name an author."

I didn't think that was a good idea. And I wasn't the kind of girl to go along with his suggestion just because he'd made it. Like, as if I were gushing, he'd adore me. "The professor mentioned 'our mission' as in *Mission Impossible*? Is that even British?"

Wythe tossed his workout towel into the bin and looked at me like I'd suggested he switch his major to literature and spend his days analyzing Chaucer. "A spy mission would be. James Bond, of course. Quite British. Finally, one I like."

Right. I Googled the author of the James Bond books. "Ian Fleming."

"You had to Google that?"

I ignored his question. "What's a good spy kind of way to do the information drop for Peppa?"

Wythe's eyes glistened. "In an Aston Martin DB5. I'll have to shower and call to have one delivered."

Such a guy answer. My funds didn't run to car deliveries. "I was thinking more of an encrypted note." I snickered. "You'll have time to shower, because good luck to whoever has to drop us a clue. They'll never get through security."

"Kira." Wythe shook his head and went to the door. "We're in the lead. We won't be getting a note."

"Right." I followed him and found his words oddly sobering and unfamiliar. I didn't spend my days in the lead. I spent them playing catch up with Felicity. Always had. Every playground, every report card. Now that she wasn't here, I was running my own race. That was...different.

"We'll drop the clue to Peppa." Wythe raised his finger

at one of the hallway guards and asked him the location of Peppa's room. I was pleased that he didn't know where her apartment was. So pleased that I decided to make the competition fair. I shot her a text message that we were on the way and asked if she could video-in her partner. It wasn't exactly spy-drop sneaky, but I wasn't a spy.

We climbed the two sets of stairs. "Why does she live here? She's not assigned to household. Heck. I don't really need to be here."

He shrugged. "Family connections."

"Ah. How English." Peppa's door was not far down from mine. I could have lived without knowing that. "Wait, I'll get some paper." I ran to my room and wrote out a hangman-style clue. To give Peppa a hint, I scribbled out the alphabet and marked through five of the letters. I took it back and showed Wythe.

He nodded and snapped a photo, shooting it off to the professor.

I knocked on Peppa's door.

Peppa opened the door in a towel. *A towel.* Like the English girl on that dry shampoo commercial, the one who didn't shampoo her hair in time for her date but was acting like she had. The towel was short, red, and tucked in at the front of her pale chest. I really didn't appreciate it. In what way was that appropriate?

Wythe blinked and backed up a step.

Whatever that meant. In hindsight, we should have gone to Vihaan's house. I handed over the paper, noticing that her hair, like her skin, was dry. "I guess you didn't get my text that we were dropping by." My tone was only a little sarcastic. If she was going to go *I'm so shocked that you caught me in the shower,* she could have at least sprinkled some water on her freckled shoulders.

I spun away. Mission accomplished.

"Wait a moment," Peppa said in a work tone.

I did not want to wait a moment, but I did it anyway.

"Vihaan and I discussed it. And we believe our team is in the lead. So, you're team two."

That made me bristle even worse than the towel. We were number one.

Peppa held out a folded piece of pink paper. "Your next clue."

I took it and strode off, waiting until we were out of Peppa's sight before looking down. The paper said, *Language is wine upon the lips.*

Wythe Googled it while we walked down the stairs. "Virginia Woolf."

I had a better quote. "My favorite is, 'One cannot think well, love well, sleep well, if one has not dined well.' Virginia Woolf." I didn't bother asking his favorite Virginia Woolf quote; I knew he wouldn't have one.

"I could eat. Let me change. Meet you here in…?"

"Thirty?"

He nodded.

I stomped down to my room to change, but by the time I got there, my mood had shifted upward. I was going to dinner with Wythe. I went with a yellow and white striped sundress and white flats. Primping took a while and I had to hurry to meet him on time. My legs were going to look awesome after all this Westminster walking.

He was there waiting. Dark slacks, white untucked shirt, hair slicked back from his shower. It made me breathless.

I leaped in with a class thought before I could flush and accidentally say something too flirty for our friendly peace treaty. "We should have thought about the next clue before giving her that puzzle. That would have been a good strategy. In front or not, we've got to think further than one clue at a time." There. That sounded like I cared about the class. And I guess I did. I didn't want Peppa to beat me. She was unpleasant. I didn't want to let Wythe down. He mattered. Ugh. I was not going down the road of that thought.

He held open the door and gave the driver the name of a restaurant. "We're going to win."

"We'd better."

That made him smile.

I got in first, and he followed me. My mind shifted back to upstairs, and my teeth clenched. What made Peppa think that was okay? "A towel. She opened the door in a towel. Who does that? Did you have some history where she thought that was acceptable?" I sounded annoyed, but I couldn't help it.

Wythe held up his hands. Pop music sounded in the car, and the driver put up the privacy screen.

"Answer me, you voyeur."

"Whoa. I'm not in control of her wardrobe." He gave me one of those side glances that said he was amused at how jealous I sounded.

I drew in a breath and vowed not to mention it again on the way to the restaurant. The evening was still light outside, I'd enjoy the historic buildings on our route, the people walking along the sidewalks…and the handsome guy who sat in the car with me. The route was less than ten minutes. The car went to the left and took us to one of those UK specialties, a restaurant that didn't look like a restaurant. A simple door with a small name outside. No flashing billboards for these folks. It looked like a private club. An entryway filled with tartan-covered furniture. Dark wood accents. Massive bar.

We went past the main area down a side hallway. It was empty. Wythe started to lead the way, and I grabbed his arm. I wanted to ask a question in private. I shouldn't ask this question, but I couldn't let it go either.

He looked down at me and arched an eyebrow.

I huffed out a sigh. "If I weren't here, would you be taking Peppa up on the offer?"

He jerked back a bit.

"Don't pretend you don't understand what she was offering." The potted fern poked my calf, making me realize that I'd almost backed into it. I stepped closer to him. "Would you be all up on that?"

His eyes lit, and he pulled me to him. His lips landed on mine. He felt right, but I pushed against him, needing answers. He moved his mouth from my lips, traced my jaw, and up to my ear. "I wouldn't," he said. "I have my eye on someone else."

His answer fixed the situation. A smile curled my lips, and I cut off the trembling, suddenly happy.

He grinned back at me. "Shall we dine well?"

I nodded.

"Do you know what 'dining well' means? Is it the obvious?" He grimaced. "Or is it some hidden poetic symbolism or something equally awful?"

I shouldn't have giggled at the dismissiveness of such a wonderful literary tool, but I did. I'd gone from low to high.

He did that for me. "I believe it means white tablecloth, silverware, china. So, I hope you picked out a great place."

"We'll see."

I sat down at the round, dark wooden table while he held my chair. I loved his manners. I wanted to know more about him. Everything. "What's in the fall for you?"

He shrugged one shoulder. "Supplemental engineering classes. This time I'll make my own selections."

We talked about jobs, our families, a sport called cricket, and travel. We'd gone through Mediterranean salads, T-Bone steaks, and now we were onto dessert. Sticky Toffee Pudding, a spongy, syrupy cake, and hot tea. We'd dined well, conversed well, and I still wanted to linger.

"If you want to do civil engineering, you should get to do that." I wanted him to have everything he wanted out of life.

He shrugged and gave a half shake of his head, like he'd puzzled it out and knew he couldn't do it, at least not now.

"Can you go to another country for engineering? Or is it one of those degrees that require specific English teachings?"

He arched his eyebrows.

"Like if you're designing a bridge in Houston, you have to take into account hurricane strength, heat, humidity…"

"I'm free to go where I like." His words said one thing, but his face said another.

It clicked for me. "How would it look if the leader's own children don't go to school in England?"

He finished off his pudding. "Not good."

"I admire your direction though. I got nothing. A Lit degree. A love of books. Anyone going to pay me to be a reader?" I took a sip of my after-dinner tea. This class or summer moving along had me thinking in a real way about what I'd be doing later.

He pursed his lips. "You could work at a publishing house. A literary agency. A kindergarten classroom. Be an audiobook narrator."

"Got it. Open my mind and see the possibilities." Publishing meant New York or the West Coast or…London.

"Don't decide. Volunteer. Intern if you can afford it. Even if you can't. Try it with various companies. How will you know what suits you if you don't?"

Actually, that was rather amazing advice—an internship at a place where I'd actually consider working. That would help me know what I want. My sister knew she wanted to work in business operations for a large corporation. And she knew what it would take to get there. Hence her MBA plan.

I'd always hemmed and hawed and stated random plans that weren't real, just to keep up. But because my plans hadn't been real, I hadn't looked into them, couldn't back them up, and didn't care about them. I'd sounded wishy-washy while my sister had sounded like a go-getter. Maybe some people could pick their one dream job at this age and have it work out. People like me had to try it before they bought it.

"That's a lot of thinking over a little statement." His accent broke apart the word "little" in a way we didn't break it with American accents.

I liked it. Most of the time he sounded normal to me, but every now and then something hit me like this. He sounded interested, and I liked his suggestion. It resonated with me. He resonated with me. "It's good. You're good for me."

"That or the fine meal is making you think well." He didn't hold out his hand and take mine. But at least he wasn't rejecting my friendship. He was being playful and redirecting me back to the class. It was something.

"Fine. Fine. Back to your game. Thinking well to me means thinking of a favorite quote. I bet that would buy us a clue. A favorite quote, by another female writer."

He stared. "I got nothing. We can Google it."

"'It is never too late to be what you might have been.' George Eliot."

"I like that one. George is a female author?"

I snickered. "George was a woman. But to be fair, I've been confused about your authors before, too. I thought Evelyn Waugh was a woman."

"She's not?"

"Nope."

We recorded our quote with the fancy dining table in the background and sent it off. We also threw in our "living literature" hashtag because I liked how it sounded. The professor's puzzles seemed to be more about understanding quotes and presenting real-life interpretations rather than truly solving clues. The richness of a long-ago author's words enriching a moment in the here and now. That defined classic.

I loved that he was opening up to me again. Talking about his future. Talking about my future. "I liked school. I did. But I need a break. Grad school isn't for me for now." I toyed with my warm teacup and then put it down in the saucer, dropping my hands to my lap. I twisted the napkin between my fingers and then looked up at his handsome face through the candlelight. "I love your work ideas for me. And I think you should intern, too. You should get an engineering job in the U.S."

He blinked.

"It's impossible here with your mom, and how can you want more school right now? I don't. Take your own advice—intern. Go for a small non-international firm. Or work for the state. Like TX-DOT, the people who do the roads." I was greedy and selfish going there. I didn't care though. I would've loved to have him move to Texas. "You'd get your work experience. Your mom wouldn't be accused of bias…" I said it all in one go and then stopped, letting him mull that over.

His jaw tightened, but his gaze was steady on me. The lack of instant denial meant he was thinking about it. The lack of flippant remarks meant he was considering it.

That made me really happy, and I floated on the thought of Wythe in America as we left the restaurant and took the quick ride home. We went through the family entrance and were climbing the steps to household level when Wythe paused. Not a kiss goodnight kind of pause, but a pause.

"That play you want to go to…*Harry Potter*."

"Yeah?"

"I got tickets for the matinee." He looked away. "We can go there. You can get your last point. We can do that instead of going to the maritime lecture."

His offer made me realize I was more concerned about being with him than getting that internship point. I shouldn't question a gift horse, but I was going to. I felt too much about this, about him, not to ask. "Why? You've been against it all summer. And then you were terrifically mad at me. Why now? Why with something I want to do?"

"You've been working hard at this class, though I know you don't want to do it. You've done it, and I'll get that point for you. You and me at the Palace Theatre."

That would do it. I'd have three solid points. I'd be considered a photo-worthy intern. The reality hit me. My heart sped up. It was everything. I'd be with him. I'd get my last point. My summer would be a total success.

I didn't plan on calling Felicity until I got that last point. It would be like jinxing it or something. This was amazing, unexpected, wonderful news. I wanted to bounce on my feet. And scream, but I didn't.

"You still in there?"

"You're sure? Scratch that." I nodded fast. "Thank you, Wythe. This internship...my sister..."

He held up his hand. "I'd rather not know."

Okay, so it was still a sore point with him. I could accept that. "Just know it matters to me."

He nodded.

I was happy. I was. But...there was a big part of me that wanted to go with him for no other reason than to be a guy and a girl out for a show. A date. A date that would end with a kiss. A date that would show him he mattered more than the internship.

"There you are," Peppa said from the top of the steps. Her position implied that she'd been waiting for us. "I found out earlier that Vihaan gave me the wrong quote for you two. A quote about dinner. Ha. As if that would be right." She rolled her gray eyes.

I looked at the big clock. It was late. Later than I'd thought it would be, nearing midnight. Wythe and I had lingered longer than I'd thought. "And you waited up to tell us?" I asked, annoyed that she was interrupting my good news, good mood, and good night with Wythe.

"I'm sure you saw the professor's texts; therefore, you know this couldn't wait."

We hadn't. Well, I hadn't; my attention had been on Wythe during and after dinner. "What's the correct information?"

"With final answers due in tomorrow, it seemed right to correct Vihaan's mistake as soon as possible." Peppa said it all in a casual voice, as if she hadn't delayed our figuring out the final clue by hours. "I didn't want you to be behind in class the way you are with the internship."

It steamed me, but the frustration wasn't unfamiliar. This kind of trick and a dig was something Felicity would have done.

Peppa must have known I was losing my patience, because she opened her palm as if preparing a speech. "'It is a truth universally acknowledged, that a single man in possession of a good fortune, must be in want of a wife.' Jane Austen." Peppa shrugged. "Sorry for the delay." She walked off.

It was not okay. I looked up at Wythe to see if he was feeling the same outrage. Wythe had that glazed literature look in his eyes.

I looked at Peppa and decided, in case she was spying on us, to annoy her. I pulled Wythe's head down so I could speak in his ear. "I got nothing. Let's sleep on it and meet in the morning."

He nodded. "After tomorrow, you'll never have to read me literature again." His tone was teasing, but he didn't really seem that thrilled.

"I promise nothing."

He gave me a slow smile, and we separated on that level so I could go up to my room.

In bed, as I turned the page on my unicorn-shape-shifting novel and relaxed into my pillow, it hit me. A great answer, which was just what I needed right now. Maybe even the ultimate literary answer. The British Library. The library had Jane Austen's desk and books by all the authors we'd been quoting. That was it.

Excitement spun through me. I knew where we'd go in the morning to finish this class, and our answer was going to be wonderful.

And Wythe would be grateful.

And we'd go to the play, and I'd get the internship point.

It would be perfect.

Chapter 19

The driver dropped us off on Euston Road right after an early lunch. We had plenty of time to get our photo and then make our way over to the theater for the play. Today was working out great. I climbed the steps to the British library, Wythe beside me. A woman in her mid-sixties rushed past us, tying a unicorn hat on her head. I paused for a second and then kept moving, I'd seen stranger things in London.

We got inside. A noisy line to the right consisted of visitors from their late teens to retired seniors, each person wearing a version of a unicorn costume. From as little as the horn on a blue-haired lady to as much as a full-fur white body costume on at least twenty of them. Most of the women wore wreaths of pink roses around their necks, making the whole lobby fragrant, and letting me know exactly who they were. They were *Hornicorn* fans.

"What's that?" Wythe stared and looked away. "Not our clue, is it? Why are they dressed like that? Why are they here?" He sounded perturbed and amused.

I shrugged like I didn't know, but I knew. It was

definitely a gathering of *Hornicorn* enthusiasts. A tingle of interest hit me. I went to the guard desk. "What's going on?" I asked, arching my eyebrows. "Is book two out?"

Wythe stared at me from beneath his eyelids.

I shifted on my feet and ignored his questioning look.

"Unicorn erotica. The author's doing a signing." The thirty-something guard had a cigarette deep voice, but he wasn't put out by the questioning. "There's no signup if you want to join them."

Heat flushed me, but I did want a copy of book two. I was almost finished with the first novel. Okay, I was rereading the good parts a second time, but I'd finish it soon. I wanted to ask what time the author would be there and if a costume of some sort were required. It looked as though it was. I tried to think of how to phrase the question.

The guard winked. "You can wait here with me if you like. I can get you to the front of the line."

I was so tempted.

"We can't stay," Wythe said. "May I ask a question?"

Just ask already, don't ask if you can ask. And we might have time to stay. Do this thing, go to the signing, then make the play. That would be quite a day.

The guard nodded, but he didn't look as enthusiastic to answer Wythe's questions as he had mine.

I turned my back on them to check out the crowd. A rolling series of "neighs" went through the group, and as people joined the line, they knocked unicorn horns. Just like in the books. It was a mandatory greeting amongst the shape-shifting sect. It identified them as human. It was like seeing my book come to life. And it gave me a fun kind of thrill.

"Where's the Jane Austen section?" Wythe asked in his deep voice.

The guard was giving him directions, but I stopped paying attention after "upper and lower ground floor" and "Sir John Ritblat gallery." Wythe could figure it out; this was his country and his lingo.

The front part of the line was doing a left-hoof side stomp, a gesture reserved for events of great celebration, like a wedding. I was so jealous.

I snapped their photo. This one would not go to the professor. He'd probably drop me a grade just for possessing a unicorn shape-shifter novel. He'd drop me two points if he knew how dirty and poorly written it was and how much I enjoyed it anyway.

"Come on." Wythe led me away. "'Where's the Jane Austen section?'" He snickered. "Words I've never said before." He looked back at the queue. "You're reading that book, aren't you?"

"Nope." I walked faster to cool my flushed face. "Come on. You're going to love the Jane Austen exhibit." When I crossed the threshold, the literary treasures caught me and drove out thoughts of embarrassment and unicorns. It was like seeing my degree come to life. Works credited to Shakespeare. Leonardo Di Vinci sketches. The Magna Carta. I wandered from one glass case to the next. Amazing. London could be really freaking amazing. This city knew to celebrate unicorns and their history all under the same roof. So cool.

"Kira." Wythe said my name in the way someone did when they'd been saying it more than once.

"Yes."

Wythe grinned. He'd never looked more handsome than he did in this room. Him, all these treasures, unicorn enthusiasts outside. There was no place I'd rather be.

"I'll bring you back, I promise. But, the quest, you know— we were thinking Jane Austen's desk would be a good ultimate spot." We'd agreed on that after a little online research on the ride over. A desk where literary works came to be.

"Yes." I went to his side. We should send in our final answer. I wasn't sad about it. It was good. Finish this class. Go to a play tonight. Life in London was awesome.

The desk itself was mahogany and small. "Incredible, isn't it? Jane Austen's desk. Does this feel right for our final answer?" I had a moment of doubt. Peppa had given us the clue, after all. Then I shook it off. Desks were where great works were created. This was a great guess. Wasn't it? Unless Peppa had somehow given us the wrong quote a second time. I wouldn't put it past her.

Wythe scrunched his face, and then grew thoughtful. "It's small. Not epic. The glass tower out there is significant though. Six stories. UV-filter protection humidity control. Let's send this, and then a picture with the tower of books."

I liked that. He was onto something. Not because of the impressive mechanics behind the book room, which enthralled him. But because all the authors we'd been talking about this summer were shelved out there together, those authors and more. It was the ultimate literature collection. "Yeah. I agree. Let's do that."

We went to the middle of the library where the massive glass tower served as the library's heart. All those books. They'd take a lifetime to read and sort. Some old, some new. What a treasure.

Wythe stared at it, and his expression held a similar awe. I knew he was impressed with the building design more than the ink on pages, but I loved that he could find something to relish here.

"Lean in with me." I turned my back to the books, and Wythe put his arm around me and tilted his head against mine. We looked like a happy couple. My eyes were a little too bright, a little too excited at being here with him. My smile faltered, and I angled the phone for the best picture.

I typed in our answer and sent it off. Nothing happened. No flash, no cheers, nothing.

It didn't feel right. Anticlimactic or something.

Wythe swiped one of his hands over the other in one of those "washing his hands of this" gestures. He looked satisfied. "We've aced this class. Now, we go to the play. You'll get your final intern point. Fair's fair."

I wanted to make the play, I did, but I couldn't shake my doubts. "I don't know. Is this what victory feels like? I don't feel like we've won. Like it's over. There's no clear finish line, champagne, or cheering crowd."

Agreement flashed on his face, but then he shook his head. "Those are very American expectations. This isn't a boat race."

"But it is sort of a race. Us against the class. I know you feel it, too."

His eyes looked like stubborn blue resistance, and then his shoulders dropped. "We've guessed wrong."

I thought so, too, and it was our last day. This was it. It wasn't the first time I found myself in this position—not a winner. And it still bit at me. I'd been naïve enough to think my luck had changed. Whether I gave a massive effort or not, I ended up coming up short.

We'd be heading to the *Harry Potter* play now, which would be awesome, but making a matinee showing didn't leave us any time to regroup here at the library. I didn't know what to say. I'd wanted to ace this for him.

The anomaly of clicking heels on library tile, a place more used to tennis shoes or comfortable flats, drew my attention to the doorway. Peppa and Vihaan walked past. Them. Again.

Wythe saw them, too. I grabbed his arm and drew him away, into a side room. This one was modern and filled with study desks. "How are they here?" I kept my voice low even though they weren't in the same room. "Even when we guess wrong, they're here."

"They got it wrong, too."

"That's not possible." They had to be following us. I knew the answer then as sure as I knew where Texas was on a map. "They're cheats. English cheats."

He stiffened.

"How else are they doing this?" I shook my head. "There was the Austen clue, sure. But it's every time. Is Peppa tracking you? Tracking me?"

Wythe strode from the room toward where we'd last seen the other couple. Peppa and Vihaan hadn't gone far; they stood in the middle of the foyer.

"Wait."

He didn't wait.

Peppa didn't even seem surprised to see us. She looked as polished and put together as she did at the house. She shifted her gaze away. Vihaan tilted his chin up. Guilty gestures. I should have seen it sooner.

"How are you here?" Wythe's tone said, *Lie to me and I will pull that rack of books down on you.*

Vihaan's gaze darted around the library as if looking for the finish line or a drink or an escape. "We figured it out. This is the place." He was fidgety, and his voice pitched high.

I didn't believe him, though it was logical. Every author was here. But it was also obvious. All the authors were here. British authors. Memorialized in print. Forever. My heartbeat sped up. I knew a better answer. I knew where we needed to go.

"Did someone on the library council tip you off to be here?" Vihaan asked, his voice deep now and rather accusing.

Wythe's expression tightened. "We came up with this on our own. How are you here?"

I needed to get Wythe away from here without them seeing.

"Is it over then?" Peppa asked, her voice annoyed. "You won then?"

"Yeah," I lied.

Vihaan's nose wrinkled, and then his expression turned faux jovial with one of those toothy smiles that didn't show in his eyes. "A win, huh? Good job, mate. Pays off to have a mom at the top, eh?"

Wythe didn't respond to the dig. "You're always right behind us," Wythe said. "How'd you choose this place? Why now?"

I wanted to hear this.

Peppa shifted, making her shoes click. "We figured it out."

That's how she was going to play it. Nothing she said

would change things anyway. We needed to leave. "I chose it because Mom took us here to see Jane Austen's desk. I thought of this place right away." I jerked my thumb toward the Austen room as I half lied. Those lies were the most believable. A little truth always sold the lie. "The Austen desk. You know. The finish line." That would move them away from us.

Vihaan's eyes gleamed. Peppa's mouth twisted.

Maybe asking for the truth would get them to go away. "What exactly led you here?" It was so improbable that they were here at the same time as us. Especially when I'd realized that the finish line wasn't really one place. It could be a different place for each team and still be right. The possibilities of literature were that varied. It was impossible for them to keep showing up in the same locations as us. They weren't doing it again.

"Sounds like you're accusing us." Vihaan drew up straight.

Obviously.

"Answer the question," Wythe said.

Vihaan shrugged. "Your man, your driver, tipped us off."

That shouldn't shock me, but it did. That went beyond cheating.

Vihan crossed his arms over his chest. "And? We all know you're the one with the real advantage. Your mom's PM, mate."

Wythe clenched his fists. A flush hit the top of his cheekbones.

Wythe's position came with as many drawbacks as it did benefits. If he'd had his wish, he'd be at a civil engineering firm right now, not a library. I moved in front of him and faced Vihaan. "Grow up. Everyone has advantages. Some are smarter, richer, faster, kinder, more talented. That's how the world works. But you work with your gifts; you don't cheat. You are cheats." It annoyed me when Peppa pointed. I figured it would bother them, too. I pointed at them. "You're not the only team I saw coming in here. You're probably in third place by now." I hadn't seen another team, but I lied so they'd go away. "Did you spot the other team? The two guys by the cello-playing unicorn?" A little detail helped flesh out a lie, and I had no problem lying to them now. They were not sneaking around after us this time.

Vihaan narrowed his eyes and looked away. "We are going to come in third." He sounded pissed and stressed.

Peppa cleared her throat. "Well. It's appropriate that we give it our all to win. It's..." Even she couldn't finish that BS. "So, another team is here? Have they been to the desk? Where is the desk exactly?"

The audacity. She wanted us to help them beat another team. I gave her a look that said exactly what I thought about that.

"We'd better be going now." Vihaan turned away, his dark eyes searching the room.

Peppa nodded. "Let's go."

That gave Wythe and me a small window to get away without them seeing and trailing us. "We need to go."

"I'll call for another car." Wythe's eyes flashed, and his voice was tight. "I won't have you in the car with a driver who'd be willing to take a bribe."

I'd think about how dangerous that was later. The risk. Well, maybe the driver just did it because it was Peppa, not a real threat. But still. The lack of ethics. The lack of fair play. The driver was straight up wrong. "No time." I pulled Wythe down, so I could whisper in his ear. "Let's take the tube to Westminster."

He looked blank. Clearly, he had no idea how to take the underground train to his own neck of the city.

My lips twisted up. "You should really go on a tour of your own city sometime. It's quite wonderful. Come on, I'll tell you my brilliant thought on the way." I hooked my arm in his.

"The guards." He wore a doubtful expression.

"Your guards should have caught the driver. I trust none of them." My words were fierce. That had nothing to do with this game.

He grinned and touched a finger to my cheek.

It froze me.

"Where are they?" Peppa's overloud voice came from the door to the gallery.

Was she already done? Though really, how long did it take to snap a selfie and send in a guess? And when they didn't get bells and whistles for their ultimate answer either, she must have figured we'd tricked her.

I liked that. It gave me a little peace in this unjust situation. She'd rather cheat than come in second place. If we took second place, at least we earned it honestly. That was something to be proud of. And weirdly, with that acceptance of not winning, I was confident we would win. "Come on." I grabbed Wythe's hand, so we could run.

"Kira?" Peppa's voice sounded out. Someone shushed her.

Obviously, I didn't answer her. We reached a long row of bookshelves. I pulled Wythe in. Maybe this wasn't the way to the underground, but we had to lose the other couple first. No way did they deserve to ride on our backs any longer. My heartbeat picked up its pace with my stealthy actions.

"Kira?" Peppa said again.

I stopped and held my finger to my lips. Standing here still with my heart pounding wasn't going to hide us. I opened a book over my face like I was reading and thrust one at Wythe.

Wythe made a strangled sound.

I looked over the top of my book. "Shh."

He was holding his book at normal reading level, which defeated the purpose, his face wasn't hidden at all. His eyebrows were arched, and his cheeks were flushed.

What the...? I dropped my gaze to the book...and it...well... Heat hit my own face. The book was titled something filthy.

He turned the page.

A tri-fold fell from the center, showing a couple in an impossible position. We were in the naughty section of the library. Heat hit me, and my mind went to heated places.

I shoved my book back, grabbed his, and returned it the shelf, too. When the library said it had over fourteen million books, a copy of every book that the UK published, they meant everything. I didn't know if I was flustered, embarrassed, or turned on. Probably all three. We were not getting caught in here.

"Come on." I drew him even deeper into the maze of bookcases. At this point, I doubted I could find our way out. But at least the titles weren't risqué. These were tomes on land masses and agriculture practices.

"Neigh."

The weird sound pulled my attention off the *Farmers' Almanac*.

I went forward.

Ahead of me, on the floor, lay a discarded pink sparkle belt entwined with a blue studded one. I picked them up. *Hornicorn* fans.

I went farther in, Wythe following.

Masquerade face masks painted as female and male unicorns lay alongside two sets of horns and one discarded rose wreath. Petals led away from the pile.

Curiouser and curiouser.

Smacking sounds sounded.

Peppa's voice came from several stacks away. "Kira, I know you're in here. I just want to talk. It would be appropriate if we sat down together. You know there's nothing with the Austen desk. Right? Kira?"

Yikes, she was close. I stiffened.

"Shhh." Some patron hushed Peppa, and I cheered them internally.

"Well, you don't understand…" Peppa argued with the patron. So like Peppa to do that.

We had no choice. We had to go deeper in or risk being spotted. I took Wythe's hand and turned the corner.

I stopped so quickly he bumped into me and had to grab me to keep from knocking me over. I didn't mind. I never minded his hands on me.

In front of us lay two abandoned full body unicorn suits.

Slapping sounds came from a row ahead.

Not angry slapping.

Sweaty body-slapping sounds… Knowledge hit me with

a weird flush as if I'd just bitten into the apple at the Garden of Eden.

Moans sounded. Soft then louder.

Oh. No.

Neighs.

Yep. I removed two books at eye level and took a peek. Two *Hornicorn* fans were going at it full speed. I fanned my face, and then shoved the books back.

I knew what had to be done.

My face was pale or heated or both, so I didn't glance at Wythe as I scooped up the discarded gear...a perfect disguise. *Sorry, fans, I have greater need today.*

Wythe, catching onto my intent right away, shook his head at me.

Oh, he was doing it. I waved my hand in a fast roll at him, conveying the urgency of the situation. *No choice. Be quick.*

We zipped on the discarded white fur unicorn bodysuits, donned the masks, and ran, carrying the other gear. He was soon ahead of me. I kept slipping on the smooth tile floor; the cloth hooves made it impossible to stay up. I slid my feet, like I was on ice skates, which gave me better purchase. I skated up to Wythe, who was far ahead of me.

He wore the suit and mask, but the blue studded belt dangled from his hand. Was that where he drew the line? The belt kept humans from seeing a unicorn's magic. No unicorn would be caught in the human world without it.

I was already warm in the suit, and the weight of the horn weighed me down. "Put it on," I said, as soon as I caught up to him. I snapped on my own, clicking the little white plastic circles into the holes, leaving sparkles on my fingers. Click. Click. Click. *Get with the program, Wythe.*

"Why? Just why?"

His tone made me fight a smile, especially as it was emerging from behind the male unicorn mask. The British weren't supposed to be fun. He was fun. "Put it on."

"I know where we are. I can get us out a side door. Or find the back."

His desperate pleas meant nothing. I had the solution. His would risk us being caught. "We'll blend in if we go out the front, past the unicorn queue. That's the best way. Like a unicorn gauntlet."

I couldn't see his face, but I saw his reluctance in the slow movements of his hands. Our golden hand-hooves covered the back of our hands and were strapped on by an elastic strap over my palms. I had full finger mobility beneath the golden hooves. "Come on, Wythe, do this, blend in, and we'll be out of here without getting spotted. Five more minutes." I fought a laugh as I pressured him.

He snapped on the belt as if he were sealing his fate. *Snap. Snap. Snap.*

I put the slightly crushed wreath of pink roses on, maneuvering it over my horn so it could settle on my shoulders. The scent of roses overpowered me.

"Only one wreath," Wythe said, his tone dry as if he were disappointed.

I didn't explain to him the gender dynamic behind the rose wreaths. "Come on." I skated away.

We rounded the corner. A lone unicorn was typing on her cell phone. She gave us a half-hearted "neigh" and tilted her head to the left so we could tap horns. I clicked with her as I passed and hit Wythe in the arm and pointed so he'd know to do the same. Clink horns and no one would notice us. Refuse to do this unicorn-world mandatory courtesy and he'd draw attention to us. Attention we didn't need.

With a sick anticipation, my pulse was speeding up at even the thought of getting to the tube station. We were so close. I put the image of the London Underground map in my head. Partly to map-out what line we'd take from King's Cross to get to Westminster. Partly to block out flashbacks of the unicorns trysting.

Wythe jogged, I slid, and we'd almost made it to the library doors. I was so close. "We're 'living literature,'" I said, exhilarated. This was unlike any day I'd ever had.

Wythe snorted.

The line of unicorns had thinned out. Only a few late stragglers were coming into the signing now. Four came through the door where'd we'd be exiting. Four horn taps and we'd be out of here, and then we could disrobe on Euston Road. Success was so close.

We passed the first guy. I leaned in. Horn tap.

Wythe did the same and moved ahead of me. He knew the drill now. He bent down so that the blonde unicorn with the oversized wreath could tap his horn. She neighed and backed up, bent her knee, and held out her hoof instead.

Her hoof!

She jiggled it.

Wythe tilted his head in confusion and his horn almost poked the third unicorn.

He raised his foot covered in the hoof cloth.

My own horn weighed a thousand pounds as I rushed to Wythe. "No!" I said, barely stopping him from touching his hoof to hers.

Chapter 20

The unicorn woman backed up, stomping on the tile in a circle, and neighing loud enough that the sound echoed in my ears.

I shoved Wythe to the door, ignoring the remaining unicorns altogether. I dragged him down the steps to the sidewalk, not even worried about slipping now. I didn't even know what I was feeling—horror, jealousy, amusement? Probably all three.

Wythe unzipped his costume as we ran and stopped at the first decent beech hedge we came to. "What?" He tossed his discarded onesie over the green border.

I did the same. Belt, suit, mask, horn, wreath of roses. The couple had really gone all out. I hoped security found these and returned them to their naked bodies, but honestly, if you're going to strip down at the public library you get what you get. Public love comes with public risks.

"What?" Wythe asked again. "Why are you still smiling? You know there's CCTV, right?"

I laughed, feeling giddy, shoved at my hair that had to be

a mess after all that gear, and pointed to the station. "The tube's just there. We're going to Westminster Abbey."

He grabbed my hand, and we hurried in and followed the signs for the Victoria line, tapping in to go through the turnstyle and then down a worn hallway to go underground.

For once, this place didn't smell like train exhaust and people because I could only smell the lingering fragrance of pink roses in my nostrils. We descended on the escalator, and I kept my gaze on the framed play posters, reining in my bubbling amusement.

"What?" Wythe asked.

I crossed my arm over my waist to hold in any more laughter. "You almost kicked hoofs. It's like…knocking boots." I giggled. "Is that a phrase that translates here?"

He scrunched his face.

I could see the meaning click, and I laughed harder.

Wythe half-smiled and touched my hair. The motion, playful and intimate, made my laughter stop. Wythe.

He dropped his hand. "What time does Westminster Abbey close?"

"Six. We'll make it."

He looked away and then back, his expression reluctant. "We can switch trains. If you like. I haven't been on the trains in a long while. But I do know how they work."

I looked around but didn't see Peppa or his driver or his guards. "Why would we do that?"

"We're not going to make it there, put in our final answer, and still make the play. No play, no intern point. Time's up."

It was English-crystal clear then, and it sobered me. I could win at class or win at the internship. Not both. I sank back against the blue cushion on the subway wall and leaned into the pole. This was it. Switch lines and go to the West End. Or continue to Westminster. Life rarely let me have two things I wanted. I had to remember that. There was always a choice, a compromise to be made. Screaming into the screeching subway car as it whooshed through the dark tunnel wouldn't change that. Even though I'd planned. Even though everything should have worked out.

Or could it still? Our glass column picture at the library was a good guess for the ultimate English literature answer. A great guess. My insides prickled. Why was I even thinking of going on to Westminster to throw another literary location at the professor? I didn't even need this class.

Wythe was looking at me as I reasoned. He didn't try to sway me either way. He was just watching me, and the reason I couldn't abandon this project before we reached the end became obvious.

Because Wythe deserved to win this. Because he was a good guy. It's who he was. And he was worth much more than my petty squabbles with my sister.

The mantle. The Christmas card. The photo.

I closed my eyes, and my stomach sank. It wasn't petty to me. Getting credit for the internship mattered for my job prospects, and it mattered to my family. And I could do it. I was close to that third point. It was a guarantee. Wythe would let me. But then he'd lose the class. He didn't care about literature. He cared about winning, especially after Vihaan had cheated. And Peppa had cheated. He'd lost his summer and his current job potential to his mom's choices. His life was so constrained by his family's choices.

I could rationalize this any way I wanted. I could truly

justify going for the intern point. But only one decision would make me able to live with myself. "I choose you." My voice sounded husky. Because, like always, choices hurt.

But saying the words lifted the weight from me, and my stomach stopped panging. My decision was made, and my insides felt good. Not guilty. Not twisty. Not conflicted. Good. Which was how doing the right thing felt.

Weird because it had been so unclear before. And now... So clear.

I looked into Wythe's eyes. "Let's go to Westminster."

He blinked, and then he grinned. He moved so he was beside me on the little bench, and I leaned into him. Who knew I'd have one of my favorite moments ever in London rocking along in the back of a subway train with my head on a guy's shoulder?

***

Marble floor, marble statues. So many royal weddings had taken place here at Westminster Abbey. Weddings. Like the Austen quote had said, "Men in possession of a fortune, needing a wife." But that was only a small part of what had sent me on the path to the Abbey.

The ultimate answer was the Poet's Corner. I led Wythe through the abbey to the Poet's Corner, where British authors were commemorated. "They're all here. All your authors, buried or memorialized forever. Amazing. Makes you proud, right? Your small island. All these amazing poets, authors, and thinkers." My voice was enthusiastic and reverent, but it didn't take much to persuade him.

The way Wythe was grinning at me, I could have said, *Take a picture of that black tile and send it in as our ultimate answer,* and he would have gone with it. He was pleased with me.

We took a selfie together at Poet's Corner and sent it in. This was our guess to the ultimate in British literary clues.

"Done." I was satisfied and content with our answer.

Wythe pulled me around to face him. "That's it. We're all in."

Gazing into his blue eyes, here, the moment felt oddly serious. "We're right. Whatever the professor says. No matter how many papers we have to write. I'm confident about what we chose."

His arms tightened, and he said nothing, but I knew he felt it too. With epic certainty. Like minds. The moment was odd. It bonded us.

He threaded his hand through my hair and absently rubbed a strand between his thumb and index finger.

Our phones beeped, and he held onto me while we checked the incoming messages.

We checked our screens.

All votes are in. The die is cast. Some teams went with volume, some with obscure facts. One team exemplified success. Kira and Wythe. Their "living literature" theme showed me they understood this project in a way no one else did. Their ultimate answer showed us all the ultimate honor our authors can obtain—to be studied, to be relished, to be remembered. While there were an infinite number of ultimate answers, they answered best.

First. My heart stopped as my mind processed the professor's words, and then the thrill went through my veins.

We'd come in first.

Wythe grabbed me and swung me around. The motion

was a rush. His arms were a rush. I laughed, ignoring the tourists and their curious gazes, ignoring anything but him and our win. When we stopped, and the world stopped spinning around me, the history, the literature, all my focus was on him. The past dropped away, and I felt with absolute certainty that I was looking at my future.

He took my hand, and we walked back to Downing Street swinging our clasped hands. Me. Him. Passing red mailboxes, shops, the bustle of people, the iconic sites. Every step in this ancient city was extraordinary.

That we could walk home from a place like that. Amazing.

We arrived back still floating on the high of our win, my heart full, and were hit by the modern and practical: security checks, guards radioing in our arrival, and an escort to the family room.

Peppa was there.

I didn't care.

The Prime Minister was there, looking like a mom waiting up for a minor. "You escaped your security detail."

I wasn't sorry.

Wythe moved away from me and over to his mom. "Really? We're going to do this here?"

The PM's face tightened further. "Peppa sorts your schedule for a reason."

Peppa came around them and stood in front of me, blocking my view, which was super annoying because while I could easily hear the lowered voice British argument going on behind her, I couldn't see their expressions. I couldn't help. "Internships officially ended at close of business today. You're not my problem anymore. You're free to your evening."

Peppa was dismissing me. "Rooms should be vacated by Sunday. You should probably go and start packing."

Wythe and I were a team, but I didn't know how to handle this situation. I moved, walking to the doorway like I was leaving.

Peppa turned back to the PM, holding a pose like a parishioner waiting for a wafer. I picked a spot where the hall opened and leaned against it to eavesdrop. I needed to understand the situation to help Wythe fix it.

"I'll have an explanation of your actions, Wythe," the Prime Minister said. "Peppa says it's been hours."

"The driver sold out my location." He looked at Peppa, and added only, "I'll have a new driver." It was a particularly English way of saying the guy had betrayed him, put him at risk, in danger…and his guards hadn't caught it.

"Your driver will be transferred." The PM nodded. "Peppa can sort it."

I wanted to yell about how the driver had taken a bribe, how Peppa had used him, but I didn't. I didn't get it, but I was following Wythe's lead on this, though I didn't understand his reaction at all. He wore a cold expression, and he didn't search me out with his gaze. It was as if crossing the threshold to this place had wiped away our partnership. Class was over. The internship was over. A hollow ache took hold in my stomach.

"The guards will be reviewed. You'll be expected here until the change can be made." The PM went to the door but turned back to him. "I'm going to need some compromise here, Wythe. An answer today. Saturday's ball?"

"I'll be in attendance."

Would he? We hadn't talked about it.

"And your date? Peppa says you haven't given a name?"

"Does she?" Wythe's voice was tight. "Well, she can just put her own name down."

What? I almost stepped out in the open at that nonsense.

The PM blinked. "Wythe."

Wythe's jaw was tight, and he was walking past his mom now, but I could still hear him. "As you said, Peppa can sort it."

Chapter 21

I didn't move. I stood there in my eavesdropping spot feeling as if the century's old floor had dissolved under me. *Peppa? Peppa!* What had just happened?

"Do sort it out, Peppa." The PM left.

Peppa came up to me, knowing exactly where I was standing. "You look so forlorn."

I swallowed and tried to blank my expression. I didn't care to have her pick over my emotions like a buzzard on the highway.

She arched her blond eyebrows. "Oh. Did you think you'd be invited Saturday? To the ball? That he'd say your name?"

I said nothing, but I blinked and felt the hollow in my stomach expand to my chest. I had to get out of there.

"You've never understood how things work here. Not truly." Her gray eyes glinted. "Balls. Westminster events. These things are for the English. You're American. You were never going to be invited."

I hadn't said I thought I would be invited. My breaths

shallowed because I couldn't get them past the bubble in my throat.

Peppa's condescending expression turned pitying. "Your duties with Wythe are complete. You may leave."

What could I say to that? Was this how it ended? Because it didn't feel like an end or closure. It made me mad and I welcomed the feeling. Anger burned away the hollow in my chest.

I knew what mattered. She and I might be done. The class might be done. The internship might be done. The summer might be done.

But Wythe and me?

We were not done.

I stomped upstairs. When I reached my door, my cell phone beeped an incoming text. Wythe. My head shook in instinctive rejection and my hand tightened on the phone. I needed to work out how to handle this. My intern duties were officially over. I didn't have to respond until I was ready to respond.

Instead of going in my room, I went down the hall and tapped on Georgiana's door. Too impatient to wait, I opened it a crack and stuck my head in.

Whoa.

The temperature of her room was chilly, and the room itself was like some freaky alternate universe version of mine. It was the "after" on an HGTV home décor show. All the décor was new and posh and pretty. It made the space seem bigger.

One more thing to dump on me today. I'd gotten a dog of a room.

"Want to come in?" Georgiana asked. She was curled up

on her little blue velvet two-seater couch, wearing pajamas and a robe, and had been typing on her phone. She set it aside at my entry.

"Just wanted to see if you were interested in going to Regent Street with me tomorrow for some shopping?"

"Oh, yes." Georgiana nodded. "For anything in particular or just retail therapy?"

"It's a secret."

Georgiana nodded harder. "Absolutely."

I was no good with secrets. I slipped in and shut the door, but I kept my voice low. "For a dress for the ball." I wiggled my fingers. "Maybe a manicure."

Georgiana blinked. "Fun," she said, and then she whispered, "Why is that a secret?"

"Because interns aren't allowed at the ball."

Georgiana pressed her lips together and looked at me, big-eyed. "Okay. Tomorrow at ten?"

"Ten it is."

***

I met her the next morning. We headed out and got manicures and lunch. It was wonderful being away from the constraints of the household and walking the streets of London, loving how the white-gray limestone buildings curved along the street and how every other alleyway held a hidden treasure, just appreciating the city.

We went to several gown stores and browsed gorgeous things. None were "the one," but there were plenty I'd be very happy to wear. All Wythe had seen me in this summer were casual clothes. The thought of dressing up had kind of an "in your face" thrill to it. Going out on a high note and the like. That's how I'd leave here. I'd relish every second of that ball, and I'd make him regret not taking me.

I held an angular peach dress in front of me and looked in the mirror. "What do you think?"

Georgiana hung the poofy green dress she was eying and came over to me, her blue eyes narrowing. "Like the length, hate the shoulders, and that would be a lot to get altered before the event." She wiggled her mouth left, then right. "If you can wait until tomorrow, I have some gowns coming to the house to look through. I know it seems risky, the day of the ball and all, but we're not that far off in size. I know there will be one in the bunch that you'll like."

The bunch? "Why are there dresses being delivered?"

She looked uncertain, and then she said, "For me. To pick from. For the ball."

The answer was confusing. She was American. Had she been invited by Wythe's brother Zane? Was it only me who wasn't invited? I fought off envy, and I didn't want to poke further. It was one of those times I wasn't sure I wanted to know the answer, so I took the easy way out and asked nothing else.

We spent the rest of the day hitting the tourist shops and talking about anything but interning. I didn't bring up the ball again.

***

The next morning, I got a text from Georgiana. *They're here. Squee. Join me.*

I wanted to see the dresses, but I also wanted to get more sleep because going to bed with unanswered questions had led to a restless night. I yawned and went down the hall to her room.

Today her room seemed smaller because it was filled with racks of dresses. I scooted around one and met Georgiana on the couch. She held out a mimosa to me.

I accepted the drink, took a sip of the champagne and OJ, and sank down beside her. "What are we in for?"

Georgiana sat straighter, and the mimosa or the champagne had her face glowing. "You're going to love them. I couldn't decide on the perfect dress. These are my final picks."

Three ladies hovered around the gowns, sorting them, fluffing them, and muttering about security wrinkling them as they'd performed their search at the gate.

Georgiana handed me a grey puffy throw blanket, and I put it over my lap. Her cold room plus the chilled drink made me shiver. My side of the hallway definitely had less air conditioning going on.

"Caroline's coming by." Georgiana wore an indulgent expression. "I told Nanny to give us an hour first. I thought we'd do the serious business of picking without her here, and then we can do measurements for the adjustments while she goes through the dresses."

She must have planned this ages ago. How was she going to the ball? "I'm sorry, Georgiana, I gotta ask... Peppa said interns wouldn't be invited. She made it very clear. So, how are you invited?"

Georgiana wrinkled her nose and tilted her mimosa glass to and fro, watching the orange liquid swirl through the crystal instead of looking at me. Her face pinked further. "Errr, how are *you* invited?"

Evasive. That made me feel weird. I clutched the puffy throw blanket, squeezing my fingers into its warmth. "I'm not invited. Not at all."

"Ohh." Georgiana made an appreciative sound and looked up. Her robin's egg eyes were big and somewhat admiring. "And you're going anyway?"

"I'm going to try. Sorry, you're as New World as me, and I was told no Americans."

"That's right." Georgiana spoke slowly and put her glass down. She scooted back on the couch, put her feet on the edge of the cushion, and wrapped her arms around her knees. "This ball is aristocracy, insiders, and English…and the hidden exception to those rules." She made air quotations around the word "exception" and then clasped her hands together.

Ohh. What was the exception?

One of the dressmakers paraded forward before I got the answer, rolling a single dress rack with a full ballgown hooked on front. She had her chin in the air and looked at us like we should bow down.

Georgiana moved back to a more ladylike pose. Feet on the floor, knees folded to the side. The formal, uncomfortable pose that was only required for bridal showers or baby showers or when I had to impress some older relative.

The second dressmaker came forward, too, motioning from us to the gowns. She seemed eager to please. "And now, Miss, the first dress is a waterfall sunshine silk with billowing ruffles like yellow waves." She motioned a third lady forward, who had another single dress rack. "And this slinky scarlet number could never hide a pocket. It says sex on a hanger."

Georgiana covered her mouth, and then whispered in my ear, "It's either sea princess or whore."

"Uh, is there any middle ground?" Because if I had to

choose, in the mood I was in, I might not make the tasteful choice.

"They are gorgeous, right miss?" The second lady said.

They were, but very different.

Georgiana and I made appropriate murmurs, and Georgiana explained that we wanted to see them all. She asked, and they obeyed. A rainbow of dresses came off the rack, and the dressmaker featured them individually for us. Each gown had a named designer, each was unique, and each was beautiful in a different way.

It was really fun, and like nothing I'd done before. Midway through, my favorite dress came out. A dreamy shade of blue. Slinky, but in a silky way.

Georgiana grabbed my arm. "That's the one for you."

I didn't know if she'd read my expression or heard it calling to me the way I did. The top was strapless. Crystals dripped from the bodice and swirled throughout the almost liquid blue skirt. It was stunning.

I could not afford that dress. I crossed my fingers. "Are these rentals?"

"My treat," Georgiana said. "I think I'm in love with the pink one... unless you wanted it?"

I shook my head. I would have picked the blue gown every day of the week. Now that we were choosing, the price tag possibilities were becoming real. Designer dresses were way beyond my price point, so much so that I wasn't even embarrassed. This had been a wonderful dream though. "These are designer dresses. I'm going to need to come up with an alternate plan."

Georgiana flushed and looked down. "Ladies, do you mind giving us a second?"

The dressmakers went back to fussing over the dresses. Despite their different demeanors, they all had the same concern for the clothes.

"The other people invited to the ball…the exception to the rules… I'm one of them." Georgiana flushed harder.

I tilted my head and I leaned in. "And that exception is…?" I really had no clue.

"The filthy rich," she whispered.

"Ah." I'd have guessed the *excessively eager* before I'd have guessed *filthy rich*.

Georgiana bit her lip, and her eyes pleaded with me not to be angry. "I didn't say anything…about my…" She shrugged. "Money. Because I don't."

I waved a hand. "I get it. I wouldn't share that info either." That kind of money belonged to people of two extremes. Those who made sure everyone knew they had bank and those who kept it private. Though redoing her room, which I was now guessing she had done, wasn't that private. But the location was secure; it wasn't like we had guests over.

Georgiana popped off the couch and held out her hands to pull me up. "Now we try them on. You can be my plus one to the ball."

"I…"

"We both know you wouldn't have gotten through security. Not here. Not at this." She grinned. "And I'll love seeing Peppa's face when you walk in."

I debated for a second. I really did. Then I smiled thanks at Georgiana. "Deal." I'd share her invitation, but I wasn't okay with her treating me to a dress. "Just the invite though."

Georgiana twirled a strand of her blonde hair between two of her fingers and checked the ends as if looking for splits. "Did you borrow clothes from your roommates in college?"

"All the time."

She dropped her hair and held open her palms. "Okay, then."

That comparison worked for me. I would have loaned her anything from my closet. She felt the same. I now had a gown and a ticket.

A sense of reality hit me—my plan was working. I was going to the ball. I let my grin widen and gave her a quick hug. "Thanks."

***

All the interns convened for the last time Saturday morning in the assembly room so some secretary for the Prime Minister could thank us for our efforts this summer. Peppa had already sent a briefing email doing the same.

I shifted and looked around the room. Did the other interns look any different, any older? Any wiser?

Was I any different?

I wasn't jetlagged. I wasn't late. Was that all I could say for myself? If I thought hard about it, I knew it wasn't. I'd seen Britain in a way I hadn't with my family. With adult, independent eyes. With a genuine new appreciation. And taking this break from my sister's emails had been enlightening…peace-giving.

Georgiana peeped around the corner, and I waved her over. She took the seat beside me and folded her hands over her knees in her perfect lady-like posture.

"Summer's over," I said. "I was not the best intern." My words came out dryly like it didn't matter.

She shrugged. "Me either."

"Are you staying on in London after this weekend?"

Georgiana looked down at her phone, tightened her grip on it, and then put it in her handbag. "There's some family stuff back home I need to attend to. I'll leave after the ball."

"Anything I can do?"

She shook her head. "It's kind of big. I'll have to figure out a way to deal with it all when I get home."

I didn't push, and we talked about home a bit, where we lived in Texas, what we missed from home. It was more and less than I expected. I missed talking to my sister more than I thought I would. But I didn't miss the negativity. I missed Texas, too—the endless blue sky, the knowing how things worked, my friends.

Peppa went to the front of the room, and the chatter and our reminiscing stopped. "Your time as interns has come to an end." Peppa spoke from the podium, and she sounded almost sad about it. She hadn't looked happy since I met her, but now she looked bummed that the summer was ending. "As former interns, you have a badge of honor to wear for the rest of your life. Honor it. The weight can be heavy some days. For any time your name is mentioned in the media, good or ill, it will be associated with this office. Every job application will ask about it. Every time. Do us proud."

The crowd clapped.

Georgiana unclipped her hair, fluffed it, and looked at the exit.

"Now, give a hand to our top interns as they proceed out to the gardens. And let's not forget those not on the top. All contributions have had value. Our thanks to every one of you as you continue on your life's journey."

We all clapped. Even those of us with just two points like me. The non-top interns. I admitted to some envy as the top interns left. But giving up the last public function, the play, to ensure Wythe did well in his class. It had been the right decision.

Though it still hurt.

Peppa caught up with us by the rear exit. "A moment, Kira."

Georgiana escaped with a small wave.

I hung back, and a flicker of hope winked inside me. It would make life simpler if I was in that photo. But it was Peppa, so those I didn't let myself hope.

Peppa stared at the open doorway rather than looking at me.

"Something you wanted?"

Peppa's mouth twisted, and she shook her head, almost looking… What was that? Guilt? She looked like Trapper did when he'd done something bad and didn't want to confess. Peppa said, "Congratulations on doing well in class."

I clasped my hands together. "Thanks."

"Well, I, uh, the interns are meeting in the garden for the photo."

No shit. It had been making me sick to my stomach from the second I woke up knowing that would be today.

"Too bad you don't get to go," Peppa said, and it wasn't said in the tone of a dig.

I couldn't even choke out the words to ask if I could. I wanted to. I wanted that photo for my parents' mantle.

Peppa shrugged one shoulder, a too-casual move that didn't suit her personality. "And about the ball…"

"I didn't even want to go to the ball." Pride put my words right out there to head off the dig she was probably building up to.

Peppa brightened. "Well, then. Good luck with the rest of everything." She walked off and didn't look back.

Super odd. I didn't know what she wanted, but it hadn't been to congratulate me. I headed back to my room. I had to prepare.

Chapter 22

I stood on the steps leading to the Downing Street gardens and saw the whole place in a different light. This was an old historic government building, yes, but its gardens were decorated with twinkle lights, and that gave the place a unique beauty. The air smelled of roses and perfume instead of tension and paperwork. The guests wore tuxedos and gowns instead of business suits.

And here I was, no longer an intern. I was dressed in the beautiful borrowed gown, and I was at a ball. Music beckoned from a twelve-piece orchestra set up on a wooden stage in front of the tablecloth-covered tables. It was a fairytale.

And I stood there on the steps.

Alone.

Dateless.

This was no dream. And now being here felt less like defiance and more a path to loneliness. Did I truly believe Wythe was here with Peppa? No. Not for a second. He'd been texting me all day. But he hadn't asked me to the ball in the texts. So I'd ignored his messages. He hadn't gone that extra mile. Set that trash can on fire. Done what had to be done to get my attention. He'd done what was expected.

I turned to leave, and the blue silk of my gown swished around my legs.

"Kira." Wythe's voice was deep. "There you are."

I turned.

Wythe stood to my right. Black tuxedo fitted to his sculpted body. Hair tamed. Eyes wild. He held out his hand. "Be my date."

Everything faded into the background, the guests, the circulating waiters. There was just cello music in my ears and the twinkle lights highlighting him. My heart thumped a ridiculous rhythm though I knew it was wrong to be so pleased at the sight of him. He was so…so…

Stop. He was here with another date. "You're here with Peppa." The words came out like I felt them, like an accusation. He didn't like Peppa; I wasn't confused about that. I was confused at the reality of this situation, though. He was not here with me, despite the fact that he was holding out his hand to me. Was it because I was convenient? I'd found my own way in, so now I was someone different than I'd been two days ago.

He dropped his hand but stayed close. "Of course not." He denied being with Peppa, but I knew he was here with her. Was he reimagining his reality with me? Like those guys who acted like they didn't have girlfriends when they did so that they could keep their options open. Ew. I'd thought so much more of him. I hated that he made me question what I knew.

A circulating waiter paused to offer me pale, fizzy champagne. I refused.

Wythe took a glass and a sip. "What kept you too busy to come see me?" His gaze swept over me from my up-do to my uncomfortable but pretty sparkling high heels. "You look stunning."

So did he. Confused pleasure flitted through me with a touch of anger. I waited for the waiter to move on before I launched back in. "You asked Peppa to the ball."

"I asked you." He shook his head and looked at me like I was a little crazy.

"I would have remembered that." My tone was dry, and I kept my insides in line, though they were going crazy with his words.

"Peppa didn't talk to you?"

"No. She came to talk to me after the meeting this morning, but she didn't say anything about any of this."

He frowned.

Was that what he was talking about? "You know, the meeting where all the top interns were praised and led outside for the intern photo while I sat and watched them go?"

He put his glass down on the stone landing, his shoulders tense. "I texted Peppa from Westminster Abbey saying we wouldn't make the play. But that you should still get your final intern point for helping me with the class. That was going to be a good surprise for you. I thought you'd come see me after the photo. You didn't."

What? I shook my head. Just *what?*

"I told my mother to put Peppa's name down to shut her up. But it gave me the idea to invite her for real. A bribe to ensure your name would be on the list, too." He was frowning, and his chest rose and fell under the tuxedo jacket.

"I went to tell you myself, but you were out with Georgiana. Peppa said she would sort it." He looked at me like I should know this. "Peppa said you'd be here. You're here."

"Georgiana got me in." My voice had weakened. I shut my eyes. It had hurt knowing the photoshoot for top interns was going on in the garden and I wouldn't be there. It had hurt, but I'd accepted it. My chest rose and fell as I let out a deep exhalation. It was upsetting to know I should have been there. That my work on the class could be recognized as Household duties. That hurt was countered by the thought that he'd tried. And he'd wanted me here at the ball.

"I take it Peppa's not as good at sorting things as we thought." His voice was tight. "I'll ensure we put someone else in charge of these things in the future." He rubbed his jaw, and his words softened. "I know I gave you a tough time about how badly you wanted the internship points. But I want you to know I understand. Finishing the internship affects your job prospects."

Heat flushed my chest, and I was glad he appeared willing to listen to me. "It's more than that. My parents were in these internships when they were my age, so having my sister and I do the same...and then putting our photos beside theirs on the mantle would have been..." I shrugged. "I don't know, honoring a family tradition."

"You really weren't in the photo today?"

"A misunderstanding, I suppose." I wasn't going to get angry with Peppa now and give that anger control of my evening. Peppa had played some game, being evasive with the truth, but I wouldn't let her in my thoughts anymore tonight. Because with his words, my outrage was morphing into something I hadn't expected to feel tonight—joy.

Peppa's manipulations hadn't defeated me. I'd shown up at the ball for my own sake rather than running home. There was a lesson in there, but I couldn't name it, not now, not here with the white lights bouncing off the shoulders of his tuxedo jacket and him looking at me with such appreciation. Not with these happy emotions bubbling through me like the champagne in his glass. I held out my hand to Wythe. "I *will* be your date tonight."

An older couple came down the steps near us, and they stopped to greet Wythe. After we said pleasantries, the couple moved on.

Wythe tugged my hand and led me around the tables, down a path, to a more private bench. I could hear the chatter of the party, the laughter, the music, but I could no longer see it. The bench was cold, and I faced him while rubbing my arms.

"There's something I need to tell you." Wythe looked away and then back at me. "We got news yesterday." He kept his voice low, which matched the shadows of this back area. "Those drills weren't drills."

My breathing stopped.

Wythe held his palms up. "You were so worried that first time in the bunker. I thought you'd leave. I thought you were safer at Downing Street with me. And, selfishly, I wanted you with me. I can tell you the truth now because arrests were made yesterday. The threat, that threat anyway, is over."

That explained a lot about this summer. Fear and relief hit me, punching me with back-to-back hard emotions. As furious as I wanted to be, it also put everything in perspective. He had been at risk. I wanted to hash out everything we hadn't talked out. But perspective didn't allow that. I let every small hurt go. This wasn't a stiff upper lip thing or some other British reaction on my part. I had no room in me for petty thoughts, not with him here, safe, and close. I reached for his hands in the cool night air. His fingers were warm against my cold ones. I shivered.

He put his right arm around me, drawing me along the bench, nearer to him. "I'm forgiven?"

"Nothing to forgive."

He kissed the side of my head and tightened his other hand over both of mine and rested them against his leg. "The intern photo. I can..."

I shook my head. "It's okay. My twin will lord it over me, because she'll have her picture up there with my parents. Just one more symbol of her coming in first. But you know..." My voice eased, and my posture eased as I spoke. I relaxed against him. "I'll look at them and remember this night, the fairy lights, the champagne, and you...and I'll smile."

He traced his fingertips over my cheek. Then he rose from the bench and pulled me up beside him. "You're not my intern anymore." He held out his arms by his side, as if in an invitation to hug him.

I moved in close and slid my arms around his neck. "You hating that?"

"I'm loving that."

There was nothing more to say. There was just a need to be close to him.

We were at the ball but secluded from the other guests. It was only us. The music rose through the hedges, and we danced there in the private dark. Being held by Wythe was an exquisite torture. Close, but not close enough. Near enough to feel the electricity but not near enough to press into it, to make it combust, not without messing up the steps of the dance. Whoever had invented slow close dancing was a cruel but brilliant master of anticipation.

I didn't want to rejoin the party. I wanted to be with him. I leaned against him but looked him in the eyes. "There's one rule I never broke that I really wanted to break." Okay, we'd broken it multiple times, but I wanted to break it more. Tonight, I wanted to smash it.

"Yeah?"

Excitement mixed with a touch of fear flitted through me. Apprehension of the unknown, sure, but that small misgiving was smothered by my real fear—the thought of missing this opportunity. Of going home without being with him. I was so sure of this decision. My certainty was like one of the crystals on my dress—solid and sparkling. "Yeah. And now that I don't work here anymore, we're not really breaking any rules."

Wythe put his hands flat on my back and my nervousness melted away. "Please tell me it's the no-touching rule."

It so was. I held his hand, and we went back to the house. It wasn't the first time we'd run down these halls together. But it was the first time we'd done it laughing, eager, and aching to get to our destination—his rooms.

Chapter 23

His bedroom was dark and quiet. Just a low bedside lamp showed the masculine blues of the décor, and a hint of his cologne lingered in the air. It was like looking at a glimpse of him. I turned back to Wythe as he closed the door, facing the vibrant reality of him.

"What are the odds of security breaking in on us?"

"Zero."

That put my last concern to rest. I raised to my tiptoes in the painful beautiful shoes and leaned into him, touching my mouth to his. "Good," I murmured against his mouth. I brushed my lips over his. Once. Twice. I opened my mouth, and his tongue touched mine. Electric. I reveled in him. He tasted like champagne, and Wythe, and the forbidden summer ball. I wanted this. The wanting curled through me the way a shot of liquor curled from my lips through my body—shocking and heated.

Kissing was wet, warm, and sexy, but it wasn't enough. I pushed at his jacket, wanting to be closer. I wanted my hands on him, the right to do that. I slid my glance from his tie to his shined shoes. He was wearing so many clothes. "Formal wear." The words sounded like a groan.

He grinned at me. "Formal wear."

It probably would've been easier for him to take his clothes off if I moved back, but I stayed close, up against him like a puzzle piece. I felt secure with him, near him, and the hardness of him appeased the aching parts of me.

He tore at his tie, and his collar loosened. I kissed his neck. Salty. Clean. Wythe.

He sucked in a breath and dropped his tie. Then his hands returned to me, roaming over the silk of my dress, across my bare shoulders.

Everything in me was zinging and tingling. This was exactly where I wanted to be. I wanted his hands on more of me.

He dropped his hands to fight his cufflinks.

I groaned.

Wythe stilled and then he worked faster. When the silver studs fell, he released his jacket and I pressed against him. My softness to his hardness. It was a relief, but then the pressure built again. The need.

He moved his hands behind my back. My zipper went down. But not fast. Slow. And then his fingertips traced my spine. I groaned again and wet my lips. He had slow hands. I thought he'd be fast because of his eager eyes. But he was slow. Back and forth. Up and down. Exploring me. Learning me like I was him.

He found my neck with his mouth, his tongue, and his teeth. Warmth, grazing bites, and licks that lit up my nerve endings. It was different when he used his mouth instead of his hands, and the electricity flowed from my neck, down my back and thighs.

It made me ache in a new, deeper, darker way.

He pulled me to him and kissed me again.

This time, he tasted a little more familiar but still with an edge of champagne and midnight. His kisses were a combination of the forbidden and the completely right—like nothing I'd ever tasted. The warmth of him, the heat, the hardness. I stretched up against him so I could reach the maximum amount of him with the most of me. The silk of my dress shifted and slipped to my waist with the motion.

"Ah."

He moaned. "Damn. You're gorgeous."

I kissed him. Teeth. Tongues. Deeper. My mind spun, and full thoughts melted to certain goal-driven words. *Bed. Me. Him.*

I walked backward, and my dress pooled at my feet. I stepped free, escaping his grasp.

Wythe groaned a different kind of groan. A needy, hungry masculine sound, but he didn't move, he just watched me.

I went to the edge of his bed and crooked my finger at him.

He strode forward and put his hands on my hips, lifting me up. It was a weird thrill to take in the way his biceps bunched, the ease with which he did it. I landed on the puffy comforter, which was cool and soft under my heated skin and held a hint of his cologne. But he didn't follow me down.

He looked at me.

I did the same, raising to my elbows for the best view.

His eyes glinted, feral and intent in a whole new way. He clicked off the lamp. The room was dark, lit only with moonlight through the sheer drapes, but that was enough to heighten the moment. I could feel my breaths.

He removed my shoes, one after the other. He slid his hands up the back of my calves. His hands were warm, large, tracing the skin behind my knees, lingering there enough to make my breath catch.

"You're soft," he said. He kept tracing upward, over the blue lace of my panties, up the catch on my bra.

He palmed my breast. One, then the other. Softly. Then a gentle pinch that made me bite my lip and hook my leg around his hip. Every new motion was better, and a torment all at the same time. A moment's relief, followed by a new more intense ache.

He tipped the lacy cup down. It was wonderful, and glorious. It was like I was sunbathing and the sunshine had reached all of me. His mouth was on my breast. Warm. Wet. He sucked, and I pulsed upward. It felt so good.

He undid the closure to reach more of me, and my chest rose and fell like I'd run here from the Thames. I was too eager, and I didn't care. I shrugged out of the bra and reached up, pulling him to me. I was all throbbing sensation.

I widened my legs, and he landed against me where I wanted, where I ached. Only his trousers and my panties separated us. I had the thought that this was beyond what I'd done before and that I should feel awkward or apart from it all, but I didn't. Being with him felt right, natural.

He cupped the side of my face with one hand and kissed me. Deep. Long. Slow. Wet. Warm. Hot. Sliding tongues. For so long that I had to turn my head to suck in a breath.

I pulled back and shoved at his shirt.

He traced his lips from my jaw down to my chest,

planting soft kisses over, and around, everywhere but where I really wanted them. He was teasing me.

I stifled a moan and tightened my thighs.

He sucked in a breath. His lips were hot and warm, and he touched my nipple with his tongue. Sliding his mouth and tasting me, teeth, and a small bite. It was satisfying, but not. Like before. Each of his actions soothed me and then heightened my torment. Blood pulsed inside me, from his mouth on my breasts to everywhere inside me. Like where I wanted him. It made me sluggish, aching, and needy.

My head dropped back against the comforter, and I closed my eyes. Too much. Not enough.

Yes.

He used his hands and his mouth, neglecting no part of me. "You feel so good. Taste so good." His voice was deep and intimate. I'd never heard it like that. I only wanted to hear it like that from now on.

I wanted to feel him, too. I got the shirt over his shoulders, trapping his arms.

I groaned.

Wythe sat up on his heels, shrugging free, and then pulled his undershirt over his head in one of those smooth guy gestures that ruffled his hair. He threw them to the floor. I wanted my hands to be what tousled his hair. I wanted to be the moonlight touching his toned body.

I was greedy and needy. I put my hands on his waist and drew patterns over his six-pack, up to his shoulders, and into his hair. He reacted to everything I did, leaning into me and copying the same gestures on me. It was like teasing, like a game, but the tingles made it so hot and sexy. I tugged his hair. He tugged mine, sending sensations through my scalp.

More.

I wanted him closer. I slid back and patted the mattress.

He leaned down and rubbed against me.

I melted and arched into him.

I found his belt buckle and touched it. I really wanted our clothes off. His. Mine. Skin to skin. Warmth. Motion. And I wanted it now. I needed it now. No more playing. I widened my knees and pressed up.

"Ah."

Wythe strangled out a curse, a gasp.

I loved it. I was tingling and heated and melted. I ached, and I wanted him closer, but his reactions made me think beyond myself. I glanced my fingertips over the warmth of his waist.

He pulled back and got rid of his clothes, then quickly returned to me, a condom packet in his hand. I appreciated that he'd taken care of it. He was with me fully on the bed. Warm. Hard. Beautiful.

He leaned into me, closer.

He made a move with his hands, touching me intimately. His mouth found mine. The intensity. My mind melted with the rest of my body as he made me ache more than I thought I could. I felt empty.

I had one goal then—get him even closer. I roamed my hands over the hard muscles of his back. I used my foot to feel his legs, hair dusted, skin rougher than mine. I had a weakness for his muffled sounds, his eyes almost rolling back, his own roaming hands. It distracted me and I gave him more.

My own actions, and the feel of him intensified my own feelings.

I needed more and faster, and harder, and now. I bit his bottom lip and pressed my mouth to his. Tongues gliding, imitating what I wanted.

His chest pressed against mine, and he slid his hand over my back, cupping my backside and squeezing me.

I grew hotter, wetter, and needier.

And then his fingers slid around to the front, under the lace of my panties, exploring me. I lost thought.

The aching was deeper, hollower, more mindless. I embodied need.

His fingers circled me, slow, then fast.

I bit his shoulder and liked him. "Wythe."

"Kira." My name sounded husky on his lips, sexy.

I pulled the lace down myself, kicking out of it, making him chuckle, until I fitted myself against him. Skin to skin.

He gasped.

I moaned.

This new intimacy was wonderful. I slid my legs around his hips and pressed up against his erection, and it was even better. Hitting right where his fingers played.

I bit my lip and then gasped, making sounds that weren't words, but that somehow told him what I wanted.

He slid one hand up, cupping my face, kissing me deeply, and then grabbed my hand, twining our fingers and squeezing. He forced my lips from my teeth and kissed me long and slow and deep, and then moved his free hand down my body. He touched me, dipped his finger in, then removed his hand. He slid into me shallowly. And then, with a deep kiss and a deeper thrust, he was right where I wanted him. I was only capable of one thought. *Him. Inside. Me.*

He'd joined me. And it was so perfect that the tears hit

my eyes, and my body throbbed, feeling full and stretched and together. Joined with the guy I was in love with. It was unbelievable.

"Kira." He said my name in a way that meant he didn't know he was uttering it. "Kira, love. Kira." My name, a breath, a groan, a promise. He pulled back and then slid forward. Back and forth.

I was warm, full, and stretched.

I needed.

He gave.

My tension built.

He circled me with his fingers as he pressed with his hips. Quick. Slow. Quick.

"Ah." I arched into him. A wave of release rushed through me, dissolving me. I fell back, and my mind went blissfully, beautifully blank. Empty of thought, worry, the world. Just peace and pulses of pleasure. Euphoria.

With a quick hard kiss on my almost too-sensitive lips, he followed me, clinging to me.

He shifted, moved. I was on cool sheets and then he was there beside me, his arms wrapped around me, facing me, holding me, keeping me while I came back together after falling apart.

"Damn." He said the word in a reverent way, a shocked way. "That was…"

He didn't finish. He didn't have to; I knew what he meant.

He brushed a strand of my hair back. "I almost wish I read poetry, so I could describe that for you."

"Put it in an equation." My voice came out husky, sexy. I kissed his shoulder, his warm, hard, beautiful skin. I licked it, bit him with a slight graze of my teeth, and breathed him in. The room, the sheets, him, they were all fragranced with my perfume, his cologne, and sex. A combination of us. Together.

"There aren't even numbers." He traced a sideways eight on my midriff.

It was infinity. The symbol made my heart clench.

"This was the longest summer of my life. Best summer of my life. Longest wait to get my hands on you," he whispered in my ear. "Killed me to wait, but it was worth it. Beyond that."

He *was* almost poetic. Living literature had rubbed off on him. I had rubbed off on him. I tightened my arms around his neck, relishing the feel of him against me, stretching, sliding enough to make his hands wander.

I loved that.

***

The moonlight turned to daybreak, and we were sweaty, sticky, and mussed, but in the hottest, sweetest way.

Wythe brushed my hair back. "Stay."

He was so gorgeous.

"I need to go clean up." My voice was super husky from sleep deprivation. Now I understood why husky voices sounded sexy. They sounded like they belonged to someone who'd been up all night doing exactly what we had been doing.

He kissed my shoulder. "Stay."

I loved the feel of his lips. I wanted them all over me. "I have a ballgown to return and a long walk past security to get to my room."

"Stay."

I loved that, I loved him, and after last night, all I wanted to do was stay curled up with him.

I slipped away. "I have to go back." I slid into my dress with more grace than on the day I met him.

Wythe got up and zipped me, sharing more melting kisses on my skin, the way I'd dreamed he'd do when we were stuck together in that closet the first day. "I'll walk you." His voice was husky, too.

"Okay." I smiled at him, too euphoric to worry about the coming walk of shame. Because it wasn't, not with him beside me.

He got dressed and took my hand.

Chapter 24

Tap. Tap. Tap.

The knock came against the door to my small Downing Street apartment. I hopped up, wearing my favorite purple eyelet sundress and my biggest smile. I flung open the door, ready to great Wythe with a...

Peppa and my sister stood in the doorway.

That brought me down from the highest euphoric peak to.... I don't know...to work thoughts and family drama. I'd hoped to never see Peppa again. And my sister... What was she even doing here? It had been so peacefully silent since I'd stopped checking her messages. I didn't want to see either of them. My insides sank. I tried to pull a social smile back on my face, but I couldn't. This was not how I wanted this morning to go. I wanted to concentrate on the ache in my body, the glow in my face, and Wythe. Nothing else. I wrapped my arms around my waist.

My sister rushed forward and hugged me, familiar perfume, familiar hug, and it was all super weird.

"You have a visitor. Visitors aren't allowed. You know

that from the packet. Security couldn't reach you. I had to go and sort it and escort her upstairs." Peppa still smelled like cucumbers and rosemary. How had she managed it? Why had she managed it? "Did your sister come to help you pack? Interns should be out by tonight. The packet said that."

I ignored her. She'd been irritating and worse all summer. She no longer had no power over me. I wouldn't pretend she did.

Felicity looked around. "You really live at Downing Street?" My sister had to be jetlagged, but she didn't look it. She must've changed at the airport because her peach halter dress wasn't crumpled, and she wore full makeup.

I ignored her question in favor of one of my own. "What are you doing here?"

"Our parents reminded me to visit the grandparents before summer's out."

Lie. Did she think I'd still fall for her crap? I arched my eyebrows. Our grandparents were British. We scheduled visits. We did not pop in. My look called her on her untruth.

Felicity shrugged and shifted on her feet. "I thought I'd surprise you."

I've never been one for surprises.

"Visitors are not allowed," Peppa said.

I wished she'd just leave.

"My sister is not deaf," Felicity said, frowning at the reminder that she was the visitor. Felicity turned from Peppa to me. She waggled her finger. "You haven't been responding to my texts."

And it had been glorious. I shrugged.

An uncertain expression crossed Felicity's face at my lack

of reaction. I'd normally be responding fiercely by now. That was our dynamic.

Felicity waved toward the room. "This is rather small. So, London, right?"

The dig didn't bother me. I hadn't spent last night here. And it had been wonderful. Dirty. Sexy. Private. Sweet. Glorious. Wonderful. "Yeah," was all I said to her. I took a seat on the chair, where I'd draped the blue ballgown before my shower. I scooted the skirt over, so it wouldn't crumple anymore. I'd be buying this dress from Georgiana. It was now tied to quite a memory. Good thing I was getting a job in the fall.

Felicity plopped down on the couch, while Peppa hovered at the door. "You're really staying here? On the property." My sister sounded both impressed and a little peeved.

I should have thought to tell her that sooner. It was special that I had gotten to stay here. Historic, really. It didn't really matter now. "Yep. This is it."

Felicity pulled out her phone. She turned it around, so I could see the screen. She stood on the top row with a ton of interns, smiling, in a perfect photo. "Here's me with the White House interns."

"Good for you."

"It was a really big deal. The White House, you know."

I really didn't care.

"Ours was, too," Peppa said. "For those who made the cut."

I'd hoped Peppa would leave, but she still stood there. Either she thought Felicity was a security risk or she wanted her gray eyes in my business.

"Good for you both." I didn't mean it or not mean it. I

knew Felicity would make the photo; it wasn't a surprise. I licked my lips and put it out there. "I didn't make the intern photo here." Then I shifted my gaze to Peppa, letting my eyes go hard enough so that she'd know I should have been included.

Peppa shifted and looked down at her feet.

Felicity smirked, not even trying to hide her gloat. She'd won; I'd come in second again.

I would say I'd learned from the British to keep my pain on the inside, and that I was keeping up this cool exterior on purpose, but I wasn't. I wasn't annoyed at the smirk. It was so weird how Felicity's smirk didn't have any power over me. If anything, it amused me. I'd done my best here. I hadn't let Wythe down as a friend. We'd ended up together, which was crazy sweet icing on a scone. I loved London. I loved him. Life was good.

Felicity eyed my blue ballgown.

I'd no doubt drawn her attention by toying with it. It was silk, how could I not? Silk, which just the night before had been turned inside out and entwined with Wythe's tuxedo. Our clothes on the floor, inside-out. Together. I felt a blush start in my cheeks, and I beat away those intimate thoughts.

"I don't recognize that dress," Felicity said. "Gorgeous. Where'd you get it? Did you buy it here?" She wanted me to fight. To defend the cost. To justify the extravagance.

There was really so much power in not engaging. Who knew? How very...freeing. I tilted my head back in the chair and just looked at her, not responding, as if her questions were uncouth or intrusive.

Tap. Tap. Tap.

Peppa opened my door.

The PM entered. Felicity and I popped up. This morning had just gotten weirder. Peppa stepped back, her gray eyes big.

Felicity knew who the PM was right away. She went to my side and elbowed me, her mouth gaping. Prime Ministers must see that look so often they start to think open-mouthed expressions were normal, like everyone had excessive whites to their eyes and showed their gums.

I introduced them.

The PM was polite but only focused on me. "I cannot thank you enough for this summer. For your contributions."

Heat crawled up my neck to my face. I hadn't been a perfect intern. I wasn't the worst. Well, with the gym's fire alarm and the dog show's alarm, I may have been the worst, but my intentions had been good.

Peppa neither contradicted the PM nor added to the PM's thanks.

"What you did for Caroline." The PM shook her head. "If I'd known a puppy would make her calm down, I would have gotten her a dog years ago." She wrinkled her nose. "They prefer cats here, and I thought when Caroline was older, and I was out of office, then she could get a dog. Who knew how much she needed a pet?" It was a politician's way of saying she'd been wrong without saying she was wrong. "She just adores little Teacup."

I was glad for Caroline. I knew what a dog meant. I was getting Trapper back when I went home.

Tap. Tap. Tap. I went over to the door. My little room couldn't really hold more guests.

Wythe.

I beamed at him. Coy was probably called for, but I beamed at him.

"Hey." Wythe grinned at me, a silly smile, a happy smile. I loved it. "You look…"

Felicity cleared her throat.

Wythe spared a glance around the room, and his smile turned to a slight frown at the crowd. I gave a quick introduction to Felicity.

"Good Morning, Wythe. I was just praising Kira here for helping out with Caroline." The PM turned to the door and looked back at me. "If there's anything I can do for you…"

I shook my head. "I have everything I need," I said, and I meant it.

Wythe held up his hand. "Recall the intern photo. Kira missed it while helping me so she wasn't in it. Arrange a reshoot."

I appreciated that he suggested it, treasured it, but I shook my head again. "It doesn't matter."

"If she doesn't care about the photo, there's no sense in calling everyone back," the PM said.

Peppa cleared her throat. "Prime Minister. There is something you need to know." She looked hard at me.

Geez. Really. Don't. Whatever mess you're trying to stir up, Peppa, just don't.

"The fraternization rule." Peppa looked at Wythe.

His face was expressionless, but his jaw had tightened, and his eyes had a hard edge.

I tried to keep my own face from flushing, but that was not possible.

Peppa cleared her throat. "The fraternization rule was broken. Between your son and Kira. They are dating." She said it like she was announcing that an overly large underground rat had crawled up to Downing Street from the river and was dripping water on the rugs.

The PM scrunched her face. "Good for you two." She frowned at Peppa. "That's really their personal business, isn't it?" The PM tapped her fingertips together. "Peppa, make that intern photo reshoot happen. But understand, Kira's getting the photo for helping Caroline." She smiled big and gave me a hug. "If she wants a photo for dating Wythe, we'll make that more of a family photo."

I stood there, not knowing what to do. Relief. Comfort. Joy. Who knew London would be so emotional for me?

The PM left.

Wythe came over to me and put his arm around my shoulders. He kissed the side of my head. "We will do that."

"I'll sort it." Peppa choked on the words. "The intern photo, that is."

Wythe squeezed my hand. "Come find me when you're done here?"

I nodded and watched him. My heart panged. How could I miss him already? I had it bad.

"He's being really nice. Probably because you aced that class at Oxford together. I could have helped him with that." Peppa went to the door. "I'll arrange the shoot. It's not really appropriate to call everyone back together at the last minute, but it looks like I'll have to."

She left, too, finally, leaving me there with my sister.

"You're going to Oxford?" Felicity said. "You're dating the Prime Minister's son? We're twins. How do I not know any of this?"

"Why do you think?"

Felicity shifted and looked away.

"I'm over the competitive thing." And I was. She'd have to engage all by herself. "I have a lot to sort out here. I'll walk you out and see you at home. You can do some sightseeing or something. We can meet up for tea before you leave."

Felicity nodded. "He is hot."

"Yeah."

Felicity left with that. No jabs.

All I'd had to do was not react to her. But I hadn't been able to do that until I was satisfied with my lot. I was more than satisfied really. I was happy. I was going to go find Wythe, and my intern photo shoot would happen. To quote Jane Austen, I was "completely, and perfectly, and incandescently happy."

***

A week later, I was packing for home and I found my paperback copy of *Hornicorn*. I'd finished it, but it wasn't really something I wanted to pass on to another reader or leave behind. Yeah, it was that embarrassing of a read. But it was a fun escape.

Wythe would be packing now, too. Or his staff would. He'd miss his staff in America. But he'd like it there. Or would he bring his staff with him? That was his concern now. I wasn't his intern anymore. I didn't know exactly what life would look like with us together in America. He'd do a job with number stuff. I'd figure out some word job to do. Then we'd meet in bed at night. I couldn't imagine anything better.

I thumped the spiral unicorn horn on the book's front cover. Ha. I flipped through the pages, looking for the section on hoof clinking and folded down the top corner, dog-earing the pertinent *Hornicorn* scene. Wythe had to see this. And I doubted he had his own copy.

I trekked downstairs to his rooms.

Tap. Tap. Tap.

I went in, waving the book.

Wythe sat in his window seat, one knee up, one leg out, his foot square on a woven daffodil.

"I thought I'd show you something."

"Absolutely." He pulled me on top of him, so I was straddling his lap. I sat back against his legs. I loved this position. It made all my insides tingle. I showed him the book.

Wythe checked out the unicorn lovers on the cover and shook his head. "No."

I thumped the spine. "Listen to me read some, and I'll give you a kiss."

His voice thickened. "A bribe?"

"If you like. It's your choice."

His mouth twitched. "Sometimes, you sound so American."

"And you always sound so British."

His fingers trailed up my forearm and he spun to the side, holding me on his lap, and rose with me. "And you like it."

His lifting me was powerful and hot. I tightened my legs around his waist and my arms around his neck. He walked us a few feet to the armchair and sat down there.

"I do like it." I curled onto his lap, holding the book up. "I love your accent. Your voice, really. Maybe even as much as you love me."

"Impossible." His blue gaze was serious and possessive.

He brushed a quick, stirring kiss against my lips.

I tapped the book on his arm before we got crazy distracted.

He looked at the cover, and he couldn't deny the recognition that flashed in his expression.

I knew I had him. I leaned into his shoulder, relaxing against him so we could both see the page at the same time.

I read to him.

Brady-corn entered the forest. The mossy undergrowth tugged at his hooves, sending shimmers of pleasures through his core and up to his horn.

Wythe groaned.

"Shush, if you're going to engage in interspecies hoof clinking at public libraries, you should understand what it means."

Wythe ran his hand over my thigh. The weight and warmth distracted me for a moment. Then I powered on.

Brady-corn said, "Aurelia-corn, you deign to meet me?"

Aurelia-corn turned her head away.

"Forgive me. The forest nymph was… Well, she was…"

I raised my head. "The forest nymph backstory was…"

"I get the gist. Go on," Wythe said, motioning to the book. "If you must." He performed a rubbing motion with his hand, moving it slowly upward. It was almost enough to make me toss the book aside. Almost. I drew in a breath.

"A mistake?" Aurelia-corn asked, feisty anger in her voice.

"She was not you. Not you," Brady-corn said passionately. "Not you. You are my mossy bed, my tavern, my cavern."

"Oh. Oh. Brady." Aurelia-corn covered her mouth with her hoof. Then, slowly, surely, she bent her left back knee, and she raised her hoof in offering.

Brady-corn stumbled forward. Eagerness rushed his body.

In one smooth, magical motion, he knocked hooves with her.

They shimmered into human form and fell upon the spongy forest ground and each other in a great tangle of unbridled passion."

"Unbridled? Really?" Wythe asked.

Humor bubbled through me. "Yep." I closed the book. "Then it goes into full dirty description as they slake their lust. So, I'll stop there."

Wythe frowned. He was so handsome.

I had to tease him. "See, so when you extended your hoof to that reader in the library, you were consenting to shimmer into human form and go at it there in the lobby."

"Yeah, I got it. But I was not agreeing to slake anything." His voice was deep and dry and amused.

"You sort of were."

"I was not."

I laughed. "Ignorance of the law is no excuse..."

Wythe pulled me closer and let his hands roam higher, making the words a challenge. "Read me some more."

Books By Emily Bow

To Play or Not to Play (Kira & Wythe) –
Romance Romp Book 1

Perfect Not Perfect (Georgiana & Zane)–
Romance Romp Book 2

A Glimpse of Us (Sterling & Chelsea)-
Romance Romp Book 3

Emily Bow writes Young Adult romance
under the pen name Emily Evans.

Acknowledgments

Considering all the quotes, I'll share another one. This one from my brother Wayne—who told me, "Stop talking about writing, and just do it." So, chase down your dreams, readers.

Thanks! You're awesome: Michelle, Gail, Teresa, Veronica, Jennifer, Stacy, Joellen, Barbie, Nash, Brennan, Joseph, Megan, Wayne, Mishann, Rachel, Darlene, Jeff, Heather, Trevor, Mom, Dad, and all my supportive aunts, uncles and cousins. I'm so lucky to have you in my life.

Thanks to the wonderful editor Tracy Seybold!
Thanks to the wonderful proofreader: Stephanie Diaz Slagle
Thanks to the wonderful proofreader: Tanya Egan Gibson
    www.tanyaegangibson.com.
Thanks to the wonderful formatters: Polgarus Studio
    www.polgarusstudio.com.

Made in the USA
Lexington, KY
08 July 2018